UNKINDNESS

OF

RAVENS

ABRA STAFFIN-WIEBE

Beware of tricksters!

Abra Staffin-Wiebe

Bimulous Books | Minneapolis

The Unkindness of Ravens

If you enjoy this book, please help other readers discover it by posting a review.

Thanks for reading!

www.aswiebe.com

Summary: The least powerful heir to the throne must survive a succession struggle and find a way to protect his people from a plague-driven war.

BISAC Category: FIC009020 **FICTION** / Fantasy / Epic

Ebook ISBN-13: 978-0-9863775-4-9
Trade Paperback ISBN-13: 978-0-9863775-5-6
Hardback ISBN-13: 978-0-9863775-6-3

Cover illustration ©2017 Scott Willhite
Title font is bu Oscar Diggs by Michael Bolen

Bimulous Books, Minneapolis, MN

ACKNOWLEDGMENTS

Thanks to Patricia C. Wrede for asking all the right questions. Thanks to Marissa Lingen for her concerns about the relationships between the characters. Thanks to Deb Combs for hunting down themes and symbolism.

And as always, thanks to my spouse Phil for creating time for me to write. Special thanks this time for reminding me that I need to make sure the important bits are actually *in* the story, not just in my brain.

CONTENTS

1

Six years ago.

ANARI ESCAPED THE Crow wing of the palace during the hottest part of the day, when most people were sleeping. His overrobe bulged in unusual places because of the knee-length quilted armor and sword hidden underneath. He assumed a bored, faintly arrogant air and held his head high as he sauntered past the guard. The guard didn't give him a second look.

Kayin was waiting for him outside the palace compound's east gate, halfway between the Crow and the Raven wings. Kayin would not risk his god's displeasure by visiting the Crow wing of the palace, though Anari had visited the Raven royal household many times. House Crow's split from House Raven had caused bad blood between Lord Crow and Lord Raven. To the gods, that blood was still fresh, even though four human generations had passed.

After they exchanged greetings, Kayin asked, "You're certain you want to have a practice bout with me? You're not up to my weight and you never will be. I was your size when I was thirteen."

"I'm ready," Anari insisted. "I've been learning."

Kayin shrugged. "I'm sure you're good—for a sixteen-year-old Crow."

"I'm ready," Anari repeated.

"To first blood?"

"These are practice swords."

"It happens. To first blood *or* to a strike that would disable in a real fight, then?"

"That's fine." Anari's nerves twanged until he released the tension with a laugh. "We did it! I didn't expect it to be this easy. Do you think anyone will notice?"

Kayin rolled his eyes. "Not unless you keep giggling like a little kid who stole a handful of coconut candy."

"I'm not a little kid!"

"I know, I know. You're almost a man."

"You'll see." Anari had been learning House Crow battle ploys. He grinned as he thought about how surprised Kayin would be, but—as he stole a glance over his shoulder—he didn't laugh out loud.

The streets stayed quiet and somnolent in the midday heat as he and Kayin walked away from the palace compound and through the city. They made it out and into the veldt without problems.

Dry yellow grass whipped Anari's calves as he followed Kayin down one of the narrow dirt trails that led away from the city.

Anari had been following Kayin since he was small. He'd always looked up to him like a brother of the same House. When Anari was young, he'd been treated as such.

No doubt it helped that they appeared similar

enough to have hatched out of the same egg. Both had jet black hair and eyes. Both had a cleft chin, a characteristic that came from their shared seed-father and not their House. Because they were the oba's heirs, neither had a House tattoo on their hand. Both had dark skin, if of different shades. Kayin's was the blue-black of House Raven. Anari's umber brown skin was a reminder of their Houses' shared heritage, not a trait preserved by Lord Crow. Their royal birthmarks weren't the same, but those were concealed by their robes.

The most notable difference was their height. Kayin was tall and strong, a man full-grown at age nineteen. Anari was much shorter, as were most of his age-group in House Crow. Every generation after Crow and Raven split, Crows grew slightly smaller as Lord Crow shaped his new House.

Still, the height difference had been easy to overlook when Anari was younger. If anything, it had helped. Only three years separated Anari and Kayin, but the other members of the royal Raven household had indulged Anari as they would a much younger child. Kayin's guide-father, Adetosoye, had even taken Anari under his wing when it became plain that he wouldn't be separated from Kayin.

Adetosoye had lectured them both, equally, on how an heir to the oba's throne should act. He'd advised them on what it meant to be a man. He'd taught them the basics of fighting. When he found them practicing those basics without permission, he'd scolded them while dangling them in mid-air without any apparent effort.

He'd given Anari his first practice sword, and he'd bellowed with laughter when Anari immediately tried to spar with Kayin.

"Like watching a fledgling try to mob a hawk!" Adetosoye had said, but his calloused hands had been gentle as he adjusted Anari's grip on the sword.

There had been other matches after, but recently Anari and Kayin hadn't sparred in months. Not since before Anari started learning the battle secrets of his House.

The sun beat down on Anari's head and shoulders, broiling him inside his robe and quilted practice armor. There was no shade. The few scraggly trees had lost most of their limbs to mourners seeking firewood to build funeral pyres on the banks of the holy Yeghra River. Even the ticks stayed out of sight in the heat of the day. The effort of keeping up with Kayin's longer strides made Anari's breath come fast.

"Last chance to change your mind." Kayin pointed ahead to a rocky hillock high enough to shield them from the city's view. "Otherwise, that's a good place. Nobody will see us behind that hill."

Still breathing hard, Anari grinned. "Good."

They stomped down a circle in the grass, tossed aside their overrobes, shook out their arms and legs to loosen their muscles, and drew their blunted practice swords. Kayin's was longer and wider.

They circled each other. Anari took cautious steps, keeping his gaze from focusing too tightly on any one thing.

"Begin!" Kayin barked. He made a wide, slow swing at Anari's shoulder.

Anari stepped back out of reach before it came close to connecting, but then he had to scramble across uneven footing to get back in the flattened circle. It made him turn his back to Kayin, who swatted him with the flat of the blade, making Anari jump.

Kayin chuckled. "Nice dodge, but don't forget that you need a way to get back in the fight, too. You put yourself at a disadvantage in bad terrain."

Anari did not make that mistake again. He darted in and out, tried for quick strikes, and worked on deflecting the power of Kayin's blows instead of attempting to counter it directly or retreating. After a few minutes of sparring under the hot sun, Anari's arms ached like he was lifting lead weights. Sweat dripped down his nose and stung his eyes. His hair was plastered to his head.

"You're quick," Kayin admitted. "That's good. It might save your life if you have the misfortune to end up on a battlefield someday."

"Why would—?"

"Enough dancing." Kayin swung his sword in a hard, wide arc that forced Anari to back up and dodge to the side to stay in the circle. "Getting tired, little Crow?"

Anari made a face to distract Kayin from what he was doing. "I guess I'm not ready after all," he said, as he pushed up the wristlet cover that concealed a wide, flat silver bracelet. His fighting instructor had given it to him only a few days earlier. He switched to a one-handed sword grip to leave his braceleted wrist free.

Some of the excitement he felt must have shown on his face, because Kayin frowned and tilted his head like a bird trying to hear a beetle burrowing in a rotten log.

Anari acted before he could figure it out. He twisted his wrist and flung a brilliant spear of reflected sunlight into Kayin's eyes.

"Ah!" Kayin flinched, his arm coming up to block the sun.

Anari lunged.

Kayin brought his arm down and knocked Anari's sword away, but not fast enough. Anari had gotten inside his guard. The force of the block knocked Anari's blade down and to the side. It was all Anari could do to hold on. He didn't control the sword's trajectory.

He heard the rasp as it snagged on the split skirt of Kayin's quilted armor, and the *riiiip* as it kept going. He felt the resistance of flesh giving way, like the feel of his knife cutting into a buffalo steak. He saw a drop of blood land on the ground in a silent puff of dust.

Kayin's face contorted in surprised pain. "Crow tricks!" he growled.

Anari regained control of his sword. He backed away. "I didn't mean to," he blurted. "It was a bad idea. I'm sorry. I'm sorry I hurt you. It's over. I didn't mean to. I'm sorry I won."

Kayin straightened, holding his sword in a guard position. His lips pressed tight with fury. His eyes were cold. "It's not over. Crow does not defeat Raven."

Kayin swung at Anari's neck.

Anari ducked. He felt his hair ripple from the breeze as the sword passed overhead. He didn't even have time to bring his weapon up into guard position before Kayin twisted his sword and brought it slicing down at Anari's ribs. Anari blocked, but the force of the strike shivered all the way to his shoulders.

Kayin attacked at the speed of rage. Instead of growing tired, he seemed to grow stronger and angrier the longer that Anari held out against him. He launched a flurry of blows that sent Anari staggering back to the edge of the grass circle. Anari panted for breath. Kayin paused for a moment. His lips curved in a skeleton of a smile, without a scrap of kindness.

He struck hard and low at Anari's leg, below the protection of the quilted coat.

Anari barely knocked the sword aside.

Kayin used the recoil from Anari's block to bring his sword up fast. He shifted his position slightly and whipped the sword straight across at Anari's throat as if to behead him.

Anari saw death coming for him. He knew that he could not bring his sword up quickly enough to block it. He let his sword fall from his hands.

The sword struck his throat in what would have been a perfectly executed beheading strike if they weren't sparring with blunted practice swords.

Tears of pain sprang from Anari's eyes as he clutched his throat with both hands.

"*That* is how you win a fight," Kayin said, in a voice cold enough to kill.

Anari struggled to draw a breath. His lungs labored, but they only pulled in a thread of air. He clawed at his throat.

"Kayin!" he tried to shout. Only a rasping mutter came out. High-pitched whistles escaped his throat as he fought for each strangled breath. Shadows danced around the edges of his vision. Anari's lungs burned with effort.

Kayin watched him struggle. When his cold gaze melted into dismayed comprehension, relief washed through Anari. Kayin was not going to stand there and watch him die. "Sit down," Kayin urged him, helping him to the ground. "Let me see—" He pried Anari's hands away from his throat. What he saw made him hiss between his teeth.

He glanced in the direction of Ayeli Asatsvyi. "Too

far," he murmured to himself. He looked Anari in the eyes. "Lay down. This is going to hurt."

He placed his hands over Anari's injury and began to chant. Anari's throat burned with a sharp, throbbing pain, as if Kayin pressed hot coals against it. Anari gurgled a scream through his ruined throat.

The pain went on and on.

Anari kept screaming after Kayin lifted his hands away. His scream floated above the veldt, loud and strong.

He sucked in a deep breath and realized that he *could* breathe. The shadows had receded from his vision. His throat no longer hurt.

"You can heal," Anari said, amazed. His voice sounded normal. "Lord Raven favors you."

"You can't tell anyone. Not in your household, and not in mine."

"But if the less-favored heirs know, they might accept exile without contesting your claim. Like—like me." It was the first time Anari had admitted out loud that Lord Crow did not favor him.

"I don't want the beaded crown."

"But why?"

Kayin laughed, a short, abrupt bark of sound. "I almost killed you, and you have to ask? You know what happened."

"The Third Danger of the Raven," Anari said. "The raven will strike without mercy to destroy his opponent, even unto pecking out the eyes of fledglings." He left off the second part. *Beware trusting him.*

"Is that what you Crows say? It is the First Temptation of the Raven: Single-Minded Pursuit of Prey. I am too inclined to it. I would make a bad oba. I would leave a trail of wreckage behind me."

"I won't tell anyone."

"Swear it to me on pain of Lord Crow's wrath."

"You're my brother! I would never betray you," Anari protested.

"We are of different Houses. We *can't* be true brothers. Swear it."

"I swear I will tell nobody, on pain of Lord Crow's wrath."

"Now swear that you will not speak of this out loud where any person could hear you, nor write it in any way, temporary or permanent."

"Did you forget to forbid me to draw a picture of it?"

"Nor draw it."

Anari swore the oath. After, he accused Kayin, "You don't trust me."

"We learn the dangers of the Crow, too."

"I wouldn't have told anyone."

"Don't forget that if you find a way around the oath, you might also find yourself facing me at the succession challenge."

"I won't forget," Anari said.

Dust puffed up around their sandals as they walked back to Ayeli Asatsvyi.

Anari stayed away from the royal Raven household for two weeks, and then it was too late. Kayin had been sent away to learn the ways of war from the Raven commander.

2

Now, six years later.

ANARI SMELLED HIS seed-father's flesh cooking on the funeral pyre. The stench of scorched hair and charred meat would never come out of the robe he wore, and flakes of ash clung to the cloth. It was his most elaborate set of palace clothing. Tailors had spent weeks embroidering the patterns on the panels of his robe and the cuffs of his trousers. House Crow priests would ritually destroy it after the funeral. Anari thought that was fitting.

The clothes belonged to his old life. He wouldn't need them in exile, because he would never set foot in his home again. Not the palace, not the country. He was resigned to that. It wasn't himself that he worried about.

The royal families of all Eight Houses ringed the funeral pyre beside the sacred Yeghra River. Dressed in their finest, they glowed like a tile mosaic washed clean by the rains. The light of the setting sun haloed the Fox priest's orange hair as he oversaw the cremation of the oba who had been born into House Fox and would return to it in death.

The holy river burned with the red and gold flames of reflected sunset, as if the oba's pyre had set fire to the world. It made a right and good memorial. Most of the people who lived in Ayeli Asatsvyi had gone to the banks of the Yeghra River to witness the funeral, and others had traveled from towns near and far.

Mourners from every House and Band stretched up and down the east bank of the river as far as Anari could see. His seed-father had been beloved by the people he ruled. The size of the crowd testified that their love had survived the sacrifices necessary for a ruler in wartime.

Even a small cluster of Scorned ones had gathered to mourn, although they sensibly stayed on the opposite bank of the river, where their presence would be less likely to anger others. Their expressions were impossible to read from so far away, but one drew Anari's attention. He was thin, and older than the others, although Anari could not have said what made him think that. The man stood as still as a statue. His pale blue robes rippled in the breeze.

"They profane the oba's funeral," hissed Anari's mother.

Anari glanced down at her. Silver threaded her hair and crow's-feet marked the corners of her eyes, the latter a testament to how often and easily she laughed. *Life is as sweet as a ripe mango*, she always said, though her own life had not always been easy. It was her nature to find the sweet in the bitter.

Now her clever fingers curved into claws as she glared across the river at the Scorned. "They make a spectacle of themselves! They wouldn't dare if our warlords were here instead of on the battlefield."

He'd never heard so much venom in her voice. He couldn't stop his muscles from tightening, but he kept his voice level as he replied. "I'm sure. Of course, they aren't the only ones."

He tilted his head toward the royal mourners from House Horse.

She followed his gaze. It took a moment for the anger to fade from her eyes, replaced by an appreciative gleam of humor. A second cousin of House Horse's royal wife had presented himself for the funeral wearing gilded archer's braces, as if he expected to join battle at any moment.

"He seems to have forgotten his bow and arrows," Anari's mother murmured.

"No doubt they are at the jeweler and he didn't wish to disrespect the memory of the oba by appearing with an inferior weapon," Anari suggested, mock-seriously.

A single snort of laughter escaped her. She quickly banished the mirth from her expression, but she once more looked like the inquisitive, lighthearted mother that Anari knew. Worry still nagged at him. Going into exile and leaving his mother behind without close family to support her was hard enough. Leaving her twisted by grief would be inconceivable.

Ululation rose and fell in waves along the river bank as the people mourned. None of the royal wives or heirs wept. Not yet.

After the oba's spirit was taken, the royal mourners would part ways. The wives would stay beside the pyre, without food or drink, until the fire died and the oba's bones cooled enough to be handled. Then they would wade into the Yeghra and release his remains to the current. Their tears would feed the holy river as it carried away the bones and ashes of the dead.

The royal heirs would restrain their sorrow at their seed-father's death until the long walk back to the palace. Each House had a different route, so that no place in the city could remain untouched by the oba's death.

The royal heir of House Hyena drew Anari's eye. Busara looked the most regal of all the heirs, but she had already announced that House Hyena would not seek the beaded crown in this generation. Her dark features were molded into a calm mask of acceptance, crowned by her tight corona of wiry, straw-blonde hair stippled with black spots.

Compared to Busara, Ahyoka appeared skittish, even though her chances of becoming the next oba were good. She had only to whisper in the ear of a horse to have it do her bidding, a clear sign that Lord Horse favored her. As Anari watched, a lovely palomino girl with white hair and pale gold skin stepped forward and eased her hand into Ahyoka's. She must be the woman Ahyoka had chosen to be her second wife. She would help bear the next generation of royal heirs if Ahyoka became oba and took husbands from the other Houses.

Anari's seed-father came from House Fox and so had taken no Fox wife when he became oba. House Locust's royal wife had produced no heirs. The heirs of House Rat and House Viper had not yet announced their intentions. Suman, Anari's protocol advisor and expert on other Houses, had heard conflicting whispers about their decisions. That left only House Raven.

Anari glanced across the pyre at House Raven. Kayin frowned back at him through a shifting sheet of fire.

The frown hit Anari like a blow.

The direction of the wind shifted. Smoke made Anari's eyes burn, and flakes of ash peppered him. He blinked tears away before they could be born. He automatically lifted his hand to brush the flakes of ash away, but stopped. The pyre still burned. More ash would follow. Acting as if he could brush it away and remain untouched would be self-delusion. He couldn't afford that, not if he wanted to stay alive.

He remembered when he'd made the mistake of telling Adetosoye that he didn't need to do exercises because he was strong enough already. Kayin's guide-father had ordered him to stand with his arms outstretched. Then he'd lectured him for an hour about the folly of mistaking his own abilities, while Anari's arms shook convulsively and sweat stung his eyes.

Afterward, he'd gone straight to Kayin to complain. They had still been on speaking terms then.

Six years had passed since Kayin moved on to a man's role and left Anari behind. The years had not been kind to Adetosoye. Anari remembered a mountain of a man, deep-voiced and solid as a rock, whose laugh drowned out all other conversations in a room.

Seen now through the pyre's smoke, the towering giant of Anari's memory dwindled to merely human. Adetosoye's short-cropped hair had turned as gray as the ash that swirled through the air. His bulk had melted away. He wore an impassive expression as he leaned on Kayin's arm, but the lines on his face were those of suffering instead of laughter.

Anari's mother must have followed the direction of his gaze. "I should never have let you spend time with Kayin when you were little," she murmured. "You still think of him as a true brother, not a rival."

"I'm no rival to him. Kayin is blessed by Lord Raven."

Anari left unspoken his own marked lack of favor from Lord Crow. Its absence was as obvious as the huge raven that followed Kayin everywhere. As if it had heard Anari's thought, the raven flapped its wings. It hopped awkwardly to the edge of the riverbank, where it used its talons and beak to pry open a clam.

"I am out of the succession," Anari reminded his mother. "I have announced that I will accept exile."

It was a horrifying fate, but one that all the royal heirs had been raised from birth to accept. In exile, Anari would have to interact with the Scorned, but the Holy Eight gave special dispensation from caste contamination to exiled royal heirs and their households. At least he would not be damned to rebirth as a Scorned one. Only if Anari attempted to return from exile would he be treated as a true Scorned one, cursed by the gods.

"You're only out of the succession if none of the other heirs believe that you are a threat," his mother replied. "Lord Crow grant that it be so. If you aren't a threat, you should be safe."

"Lord Crow has never granted me any favors," he said bitterly. As soon as the words escaped his mouth, he wished he could call them back. You never knew when the gods were listening and might take offense. When the god of your House was a trickster, you needed to take extra care.

They fell silent as the Fox priest raised a long pole above his head. The sky behind the priest burned orange and red. After holding the pole aloft for the space of three heartbeats, he brought it whistling down to strike the forehead of the dead oba.

The *crack* of the skull splitting resounded in the silence left by hundreds of people holding their breath. Even the Yeghra River seemed muted.

A burst of flame roared up from the body. The priest tossed the pole onto the pyre and stepped back. He looked diminished, an ordinary man instead of the emissary of his god. His hair was still orange, but it no longer blazed like fire.

A chill went through Anari as he looked around at the circle of royal mourners and their households. Without the power of the gods flowing through them, the priests returned to being simple members of their Houses. Only the royal heirs could channel the power of the gods now, and even then, only to the extent that their personal connection to their Lord or Lady allowed. Until a new oba wore the beaded crown, the priests could not sanction births, invoke war blessings, or heal so much as a scratch. In battle or by accident, people would die who could have been saved.

Anari glanced down at his mother and caught her angrily dashing tears from her eyes. His worry for her returned. "Mother—?"

"Go. It is time," she said, still facing the burning pyre. "Take the household back to the palace. You know the Crow route."

"Will you be all right?"

"I will be fine with the other wives. We will walk back after we've given his bones to the Yeghra."

"Do you need anything?" He felt compelled to ask, though he couldn't give her food or drink or even a mat to sit on.

She met his eyes then. Her own were bright with banished tears. "I don't grieve my husband, I fear losing my son. Go quickly. Be careful. Trust no-one."

The Scorned on the other side of the river were drifting away. The thin Scorned one in the blue robes was nowhere to be seen. Anari frowned at their disrespect in daring to leave before the royal families.

The rest of the mourners would trickle back into the city after the royal households had passed. House Rat had already vanished, but the other House processions were still assembling. Anari gestured to his household and picked up his pace, hoping to get underway before the rest of the Houses. The warmth of the setting sun painted a target on Anari's back as he led the Crow procession away from the smoldering pyre at the river's edge.

A zigzagging dirt path rose from the edge of the river to the regular city streets. As Anari walked up it, the muffled footsteps of his household trailed him like ghosts. Behind him, he heard the royal wives begin to wail their grief. He couldn't tell which voice belonged to his mother.

When he reached the street, his mind blanked. He knew that he knew the way. Yet in that moment, the memory was as distant as a dream of flying on crow's wings. He stumbled. Sweat trickled down his spine and pooled in the small of his back.

"Eye," said the Crow doorkeeper, using Anari's title.

That one word snapped Anari back to himself. He was the Eye of House Crow, the royal heir. He would do this. House Crow took the widest path, the one that would split into five forks before rejoining at the end.

Anari led the way. Every time the path forked, the Crow royal household also split. They would travel in small groups of two or three through the city before coming back together in a giant muster, the way that all the crows in the city came together to roost during the dry season.

Only a few people had remained in Ayeli Asatsvyi: the elderly, the bedridden, the indispensable, and the otherwise indisposed. Anari and his flock traveled through abandoned streets flanked by shuttered shops and barred doors.

As Anari stalked down the street, he drew his dagger and hooked the curved end over the shoulder seam on his robe. He drew a deep breath and slashed through the seam, dragging his dagger diagonally across his chest.

"*Yaaaaaaa!*" he screamed.

He screamed his grief for the seed-father he'd barely known, whose influence had stretched across every moment of his life. He shouted his anger at the competition to become the new ruler and at his inevitable failure. He cried his fear of a life in exile, surrounded by an ocean of Scorned ones. He raged at his powerlessness to protect those he would leave behind.

With every step, he cut and tore his garments, until his fine embroidered robe and trousers were shredded into rag strips that danced as he walked. Only his loincloth protected his dignity. A thin line of red grew across his chest where he had cut too deep. He screamed and wailed until his throat was burned raw and his soul numb and he could lament no more.

The world crept back into the space left by his silence. He heard footsteps behind him. When he glanced over his shoulder, he saw the small flock who followed him: the head cook, one of the junior sweepers, and his protocol adviser, Suman. He hadn't heard any other voices over the sound of his own grief, but now their ritual lamentations echoed through the streets.

When they entered the bazaar, Anari saw in a glance that they were the first of royal House Crow to arrive at the gathering place. He nodded in approval. As it should be. A patchwork of branch roofs, canvas canopies, and ragged blankets shaded the bazaar. Nothing moved in the forest of stalls except an unsecured corner of canvas flapping against a wooden post.

A lone man sat on a stool in front of a shuttered tea shop nearby. As Anari watched, the man picked up a grass broom and leaned over to give the shop's threshold a desultory swipe. A tall clay water pot stood beside the door. The dirt packed around its base was dark with moisture. Anari swallowed hard. His throat was parched. He felt every throat-tearing scream of grief he'd uttered.

The day's heat had passed, but the night's cool blessing hadn't yet reached Ayeli Asatsvyi. Sweat plastered Anari's tattered robes to his body. Grainy fragments of ash itched in the folds of his skin. He longed for the purifying bath that awaited him in the palace.

A blue ceramic tile with a crow in flight sat above the mantel of the tea shop's door, showing their connection to House Crow. Surely they would not begrudge a scoop of water to the Crow royal heir.

The man in front of the shop did not immediately rise to his feet as Anari approached. He stayed seated, his hands tucked into the pockets of his robe. Annoyance flickered through Anari until he saw the reason. The man's right shoe cradled a wooden foot, and the outline of a leg brace was visible under his trouser leg.

Still, Anari wouldn't be careless about his approach. *Trust no-one*, his mother had said.

He sheathed the dagger that he'd used to tear his mourning clothes, but he remained poised to leap back and draw it again, in case this was an elaborate ruse to disarm him.

"Greetings to you," Anari said, extending his right hand for the ritual handclasp.

The man struggled to his feet. He took Anari's hand awkwardly with his unmarked left hand.

Anari bristled at the insult.

"My apologies, but I lost my hand in battle." He showed Anari the stump of his right wrist. "Hiran of Band Starling," he introduced himself. "Smooth your feathers, young Crow."

Band Starling was one of the largest Bands in House Crow. Anari relaxed, and he felt the others behind him do the same. House tattoo or not, nobody would dare claim a false House when the gods might be listening. He drew reassurance from the familiar jet black hair and eyes as he looked up at the older man.

"Anari of House Crow," Anari introduced himself. He glanced at the water pot. "You have a good situation, Hiran. On hot days, it must be a blessing to have cool drinking water so close."

"Oh, yes," Hiran agreed. "You are on the mourner's walk?"

Anari nodded.

"The walk is hard. I remember when the old oba returned to House Hyena. We followed the procession of royal mourners all the way back to the palace. I was so thirsty, and my feet hurt so much." He waved his grass broom in the direction of his right foot. "I still had both the originals then. I never thought I'd miss having my feet hurt," Hiran mused. "I knew I wasn't going to go for the priesthood, you see. Back then, the only people with missing limbs were the ones with a sacred calling who had sacrificed their flesh to gain the favor of the gods."

Anari nodded. He didn't remember much about how things were before the war started, but the older generations loved to talk about it. His attention drifted to the bazaar entrances where he expected the rest of his household to appear, but he kept his face politely attentive. He thought he heard footsteps in the distance.

Hiran must have sensed his distraction, or perhaps he heard the footsteps too. "Enough of my rambling! I remember how much I wanted a cup of cold drinking water that day."

Anari swallowed hard against the sandpaper rasp of his throat.

"I can do that much for you. Come." Hiran limped over to the tall clay water pot, lifted the tray covering the pot's mouth, and drew out a ladle of cool water. Drops rolled down the sides of the ladle and splattered in the dust. "No cup, I'm afraid."

"Eye!" called Suman, House Crow's protocol advisor. "I hear the others coming."

"Then I will be refreshed when they arrive," Anari said. He cupped his hands, and Hiran poured the water into them.

"Drink up," Hiran said. "The owner of the tea shop won't begrudge it."

Hiran's phrasing rang strangely in Anari's ears. It nagged at Anari as he lifted his hands to drink.

The cold water could have been poured straight from one of the heavenly rivers. It kissed his chapped lips and blessed his aching throat as he swallowed. The water tasted sweet, sweet, despite traces of gritty ash from his palms.

"I must check the back door of the shop and make sure everything is in order," Hiran excused himself. He limped away.

The owner of the tea shop. That was not how a hired door sweeper would talk about the person who gave them that position. They would say, "My boss." If they felt a strong allegiance, they would say *Uncle* or *Auntie*, whether or not they were linked by a blood bond tighter than a shared House.

That lingering oversweet aftertaste wasn't because Anari was so thirsty. The wave of dizziness crashing over him wasn't because he was exhausted from walking. Hiran wasn't leaving to check the shop's back door.

He was escaping because he'd attempted to murder a royal heir.

"Stop him!" Anari shouted, or tried to shout. It came out as a whisper with no force behind it. He raised his hand to point and stared in horror at the tremors shaking it.

Sharp pain knifed his stomach. He doubled over, lost his balance, and would have fallen if he hadn't slapped his hand down on the ground in front of him. Nausea seized him. Bitter vomit burned its way up his throat and splashed across the hard-packed dirt. Droplets freckled his hand. The acrid smell caused him to retch again, helplessly. The scalding pain in his throat brought tears to his eyes. Snot dripped from his nose and ran down his chin.

It didn't matter. All that mattered was not falling over, no matter how the world spun. He locked his gaze on a crack in the ground. As long as kept his eyes on the crack, he would not fall over.

Voices swarmed around him. Running footsteps drummed through the streets. A red velvet mite trundled along beside the crack in the ground. The hairs on its back looked so soft.

Blink. He was laying on his back in the street. Other members of the Crow royal household had reached the meeting place. They huddled around him. Their faces looked strange when seen from below, their expressions distorted. Pain radiated from Anari's stomach to every muscle in his body. His back arched.

"Turn him on his side so he doesn't choke!" That was their House's healer priest, Romesh. He pressed three fingers to Anari's wrist, taking his pulse. "I need to get him to my workroom as fast as possible. You!" He released Anari's wrist to point to someone buried in the crowd. "Run to the stables and get a war horse strong enough to carry two. Fly!"

Light, quick footsteps faded into the distance.

"Heal him!" cried the junior sweeper. "Why don't you heal him?"

The cook put an arm around the junior sweeper's shoulders. "The oba is dead. There is no healing to be had. The priests can't reach the gods."

Anari had guarded against deadly weapons. He hadn't guarded against this, because who would use poison when a single visit to a healer priest could undo the damage? He'd forgotten the Fourth Temptation of the Crow: Expectations. He had expected people to behave the same way, even when circumstances changed. Now he suffered for it.

Blink. He was upright, his arms stretched over the shoulders of two of the burliest men in his household.

His feet dragged in the dirt behind them. One foot snagged on a rut in the street, pulling his body straight. A white sheet of pain washed over him.

Blink. The ground was very far away. He sat on a horse's bare back. Someone sat behind him and held him in place.

"Hold him up! Tie the sash around his chest. Tight."

Blink. Every hoof-strike reverberated through his gut as if the horse trotted across his body instead of the street.

"We're almost there," Romesh said behind him, close to his ear.

"Eye of House Crow! I must speak to you!"

The horse snorted and reared its head as a man dashed into the street before them in a flurry of light blue robes. Only the war horse's meticulous training kept it from shying away.

"Out of the way!" Romesh ordered.

The blue robes were old and stained, patched with coarser cloth than the original. Who would be so disrespectful as to wear such rags on the day of the oba's funeral?

The man seized the reins, pulling the horse's head down.

"Eye, I must speak to you!" he insisted.

He was a thin older man with an accent, a strange burnished brass cast to his skin, and lines of bitter suffering on his face. It was the sight of his unmarked hand holding the reins that reminded Anari of where he'd recently seen a thin older man in light blue robes. Shock cut through the pain fogging Anari's thoughts.

"Watch out—Scorned," Anari whispered.

A sharp intake of breath from behind him said

that Romesh had heard him. Good. He could let Romesh handle it. He focused on the pain radiating from his abdomen, trying to imagine it outside of himself.

"Please, hear me!" The Scorned one reached toward them.

Romesh jerked the reins away from the Scorned one and ordered, "Strike."

The war horse reared and kicked out with its front legs, knocking the Scorned one to the ground in front of them. The movement sent Anari rocking back. He thudded against Romesh's chest, nearly knocking them both off the horse. Romesh grabbed Anari and curled forward to keep them on the horse.

Anari gasped as the pain in his abdomen expanded like a lake overflowing in the rainy season. He swayed. His head lolled against his chest. Darkness hovered at the edges of his vision. He stared down at the ground as glimpses of blue robes and horse hooves danced in and out of view. Only the sash tied around his chest kept him semi-upright.

"Gallop," Romesh ordered tightly.

The war horse's hooves plunged down. The Scorned one tried to scrabble out of the way.

He didn't quite make it.

One sharp-edged hoof landed on his hand with a muffled cracking sound. He screamed the high-pitched, throat-scraping scream of someone in unendurable pain. The burst flesh of his hand curled up around the edge of the horse's hoof. His fingers twitched and splayed like the legs of a dying spider.

The horse stretched its legs into a gallop, leaving the screaming behind. The blows of its hooves echoed through Anari's body. Blackness swept across his vision.

Blink.

"Help me get him inside. Hold him while I untie the sash."

Hands seized him around the waist. He arched his back and screamed.

Blink. He stared up at a familiar ceiling. A wave of painful nausea rolled through him. A whimper escaped between his teeth. He tasted acid rising in the back of his throat.

Romesh loomed above him. "Eye, I am happy to see that you are awake. Let me help you sit up. This will hurt," he warned. "There is no shame in screaming. Try not to faint. You must be aware to drink this preparation."

He hooked his arms under Anari's armpits and heaved him into a sitting position on the rope bed. Anari clung to consciousness. He had no shame.

When he stopped screaming, the nausea surged back up his throat. A bowl appeared in front of him just in time. He retched thin, sour-tasting strings of vomit. Romesh held the bowl until Anari ran dry, although his body still spasmed and shook.

"This is good. Before taking the preparation, the more you vomit, the better."

Anari leaned stiffly against the cushions piled behind him. All the muscles in his back were locked tight, as if he could keep the pain away by holding himself in precisely the correct position.

Romesh lifted a tin cup to Anari's lips. Murky gray-black liquid swirled inside the cup. Anari gulped it down between waves of nausea. It left his mouth tasting of ashes.

They waited, Romesh with bowl in hand. Anari's muscles stayed locked in pain, but slowly he felt the urge to vomit subside. When he told Romesh this, the healer priest looked relieved.

Romesh lifted Anari's hands and studied his nails. He asked him to open his mouth and checked the color of his lips and gums. He tapped and palpated his way along Anari's body before pronouncing his verdict.

"The treatment is working. The preparation you swallowed will prevent your body from absorbing the rest of the poison. I regret that I can give you nothing for the pain, but your body would not absorb it either. According to the notes, the way you feel is to be expected."

"According to the notes?" Anari rasped.

"I was not yet a healer when the previous oba returned to her House. This is the first time I've had to treat patients without the blessing of Lord Crow. Once it became clear that our oba had the rotting lung sickness and would die, I began studying previous healers' notes on how to preserve patients through the changeover. I prepared everything I could for my workroom, and I sent what I could come up with for war wounds to the Crow chief healer at the battlefront."

Anari grunted an acknowledgement.

Romesh sighed. "The battle healers ran through the supplies I sent in a matter of days. Without war blessings, our warriors cannot defend themselves against the flood of infidels crossing the desert land bridge. Our warriors are being pushed back. We've lost many to death or injury."

The bald statement struck Anari like a blow. The royal heirs of the Eight Houses were raised to protect their people. That was one place that the lessons of House Crow and House Raven were in perfect agreement. All the royal heirs knew that one day they might become oba. Then the walls that bound them to one god and one House would shatter, and all the people in the land would become theirs to protect. Now all those people were in danger, and Anari could do nothing. That Romesh didn't blame him made it worse.

Sweat beaded along Anari's hairline. He groaned.

Romesh readied the vomit bowl.

Anari shook his head. At the motion, pain spiked from his skull to the base of his neck. His eyes closed involuntarily, but that left him with nothing to distract from the pain. He forced himself to open his eyes, to think.

Romesh set aside the vomit bowl and gestured to a row of covered baskets and large clay pots lined up along the wall. "I'm sending this shipment the day after tomorrow. It won't last long."

"How did you know the oba would die?" Anari asked. "People have survived rotting lung sickness. Guang the Fearless had rotting lung sickness as a youth, but he went on to win great victories."

Romesh shook his head. "He was healed during the cascade when the gods flooded a new oba who belonged to his house, an oba who was also a healer. It would have been possible at no other time."

A wave of pain sent spots dancing in front of Anari's eyes. He groaned. "The notes say the treatment should hurt ... this much?"

"Some portion of the poison affected you before I could give you the preparation. You're young and strong. You should live. Any lingering damage can be healed once there is a new oba."

"Even though—even if the oba is not from House

Crow?"

Romesh nodded. "I'll be able to heal again. That will be enough for this, even if we should happen not to receive the cascade that passes through the oba to their former House."

It was kind of him not to mention that the poisoning itself proved Anari didn't have a special connection to Lord Crow and wasn't worthy of being oba. There had been no warning from Lord Crow. No special sense that anything was amiss. No crow cawing a warning from a rooftop. Not even a splatter of white bird droppings to mark the ladle as not good to drink from. That was how little Lord Crow valued his life.

If Anari died, nobody would hunt his killer. If he'd been meant to live, Lord Crow would have protected him.

Hiran's attempt to murder him would be forgiven. But he had committed a worse crime in claiming to be of Band Starling, House Crow. The gods would turn their faces from him, the priests would cast him out of his House, and he would be reborn Scorned in his next turn on the wheel, so that all would know he was not to be trusted.

"There is still poison in you," Romesh told him. "It is affecting your organs and upsetting the elemental balance in your body."

A surge of pain twisted through Anari, as if to remind him that he might still die. He panted through the pain. After it had subsided, he said, "If you'd needed to go to a Crow temple for purification before you could treat me …"

Romesh nodded. "If I had been polluted, unable to act as a healer and give you the preparation, you would likely be dead."

Anari remembered the Scorned one reaching for them. He shuddered. "You did well to ask for a war horse."

"Thank you, Eye. I was only thinking of the strength a horse needed to carry two. I did not expect anyone to be foolish enough to attempt to stop us, much less a Scorned one."

"Who would have? What could have driven him to such a mad act?"

Romesh shrugged. "The Scorned don't think in the same way that you or I do. Don't waste your energy lowering yourself to try and understand them. Save your strength. We must return your body to balance through cleansing and bloodletting."

3

WHEN ANARI OPENED his eyes, he relished the feeling of rising slowly from natural slumber to consciousness. He stared at the mural of lilies and lotus flowers on his bedroom ceiling and wondered why he was so happy to see it. He turned his head to the side and saw the wooden boxes filled with his personal belongings stacked against his wall, ready for him to take into exile.

He remembered weirdly blurred, disconnected fragments, like a fight seen through shifting smoke. He was happy to see his ceiling because ... it was not the ceiling in Romesh's workroom. He was in his own bed. His stomach no longer hurt like he'd swallowed burning coals. The echo of that pain dispelled the smoke clouding his mind, and his memories sprang into deadly sharp focus.

He groaned.

The noise spurred a flurry of motion near the doorway to his room. A young Crow pushed himself up from the straw mat he'd been napping on. "You're awake! I will get Romesh. Please lie still. He said to tell you that."

Before Anari could respond or extend his hand in greeting, the boy darted out of the room.

Anari gripped the edges of his bed and pulled himself up to a sitting position. His arms trembled. Tiny shocks of pain sparked with every movement. He let his head sag.

He looked up at the sound of footsteps returning in haste. The Crow boy returned with Romesh on his heels.

Romesh hissed through his teeth when he saw Anari sitting upright, but he didn't chastise him. "Eye, I am happy to see you. How do you feel?"

When nobody gave the Crow boy any further orders, he ducked out of the room.

Anari's fingers brushed Romesh's House Crow tattoo as they gripped hands in greeting. He took strength from the reminder that he was among his House.

"My limbs are weak. Everything hurts, but not the way it did before. This is like the pain of a fresh bruise. No, dozens of fresh bruises! The pain moves when I do. Tell me, how long did I sleep?"

"You slept through the night and the whole day. The evening flame has already been offered to Lord Crow. You've missed four meals, which is good. Fasting will help you purify yourself. Let me take your pulse."

Anari allowed Romesh to place three fingers on his wrist. "So I have five days until the new oba must stand before the gods. The mourning ceremony has finished? My mother has returned home safely?"

"Yes, she took the widow's walk back from the holy river with the other wives. She felt a little weak and dizzy on the walk, but that is to be expected with fasting. She recovered her strength as soon as she drank a large cup of milk and ate some dates."

"What news has come from the other Houses?"

"I hesitate to say. I devoted myself to your care. I only left your room to sleep for a couple of hours after the worst of the effects seemed to have passed."

Which meant that Anari wasn't going to die anytime soon and still had to worry about problems like avoiding another assassination attempt. He needed to know more.

"Where did the boy go?" Anari asked.

"Gati!" Romesh called.

The boy stuck his head around the corner of the door. "Yes, Uncle?"

"Gati," Anari said, "I need you to summon my protocol advisor Suman, the head sweep, and Dai Kalinda for me. Have the head sweeper also send a junior sweeper immediately to take that away." He pointed to the squatting pan.

"Yes, Eye."

Anari eased back onto the bed. With Romesh's help and several strategically placed cushions, he arranged himself in something approximating a sitting position while he waited.

After the others arrived and exchanged handclasps and greetings, Anari spoke first to the dai priest. "Dai Kalinda, I need to know if Lord Crow sanctioned the birth of a boy named Hiran to Band Starling."

She didn't answer immediately. "How old is he? There is a five-year-old …"

"He said he was my age or a little older when the old oba returned to House Hyena, so he would be of my mother's generation." Hiran had lied about many things, but that memory had held the ring of truth. "He was missing a hand and a foot."

"I wouldn't know what happens to the children when they are grown unless they return to petition Lord Crow for a child of their own. A moment." Dai Kalinda closed her eyes. Her lips moved silently as she recited the list of sanctioned births. She opened her eyes. "No, not in all of House Crow. Hiresh is the closest name."

"Thank you. Do you know the names of the children sanctioned by other gods?" he asked, even though he thought he knew what her answer would be.

"Only if their seed-father or milk-mother is of House Crow, but Hiran is a House name. No child of another house would use it."

"He lied about his name. Even so, a man of that age missing a hand and a foot could not hide forever in House Crow." A shock of revulsion traveled through Anari. "He must have lied about his House."

Dai Kalinda gasped. "How is that possible?"

"He lost his House tattoo along with his hand, or so he said."

"But—the gods will cast him out for that sacrilege. He will live the rest of this life and the next Scorned. He will be reborn with mixed House traits, so he can never deceive anyone in that way again." She shuddered. "That he dared to commit such blasphemy! Could he already be Scorned? He might have struck off his own hand to conceal the lack of a tattoo."

"No," Anari's protocol advisor Suman answered her fear. "The Scorned would not dare. They know it would only make their lives worse. House priests would hunt them down and speed them on to the next turn of the wheel. The gods would see to it that they were reborn as an animal or an insect, lower even than the

Scorned. If a Scorned one had ever attempted such a ruse, I would have heard of it. Everyone would have."

She didn't look entirely convinced. "But what if they were not caught?"

"He would have had to chop off his hand for the ruse. Scorned ones don't have the courage to make that kind of sacrifice," Anari added, to reassure her. He turned to his protocol advisor. "Suman, have there been any declarations from the other Houses?"

Suman bowed his head. "House Hyena has announced the death of the Hyena royal heir."

"But Busara said she would not seek the beaded crown." Anari remembered how calm and regal she had appeared at their seed-father's funeral.

"So did you," Suman replied. "Whoever is behind this is taking no chances."

"Bandhu, what gossip have your people heard about the succession?" Anari asked the head sweeper. Sweepers worked inside and outside the Crow royal wing of the palace. Often higher-ranked people spoke in front of them as if they weren't there. Anari would never make that mistake, not after growing up sitting at his mother's feet while she interrogated the sweepers for gossip from the other royal households.

"Tawil of House Rat has vanished," Bandhu said.

"Dead?"

Bandhu tilted his head in a maybe-yes, maybe-no gesture. "He has disappeared so thoroughly that most of his household has no idea."

"Any other news?"

Bandhu considered. "Perhaps. Ahyoka has a magnificent new mare. The stable sweeps weren't warned that there would be a new horse arriving."

"And?"

"She finished the mourner's walk on horseback."

Lord Horse had sent a messenger to warn Ahyoka of a threat. Anari swallowed bitterness that Lord Crow had not bothered to do the same for him.

"Is there any other news? What of House Raven?" he couldn't help asking. Seeing Kayin through the smoke of their seed-father's pyre had broken open an old wound.

"I have heard no gossip from House Raven," Bandhu answered.

"Suman?"

"House Raven has made no announcements," Suman said carefully.

Anari's attention sharpened at his tone. "Why do you say it like that?" he demanded.

Instead of answering, Suman turned the questioning back on him. "Have you finished your other inquiries?"

Anari narrowed his eyes. "Yes. Thank you," he told the others. "My need of you is done."

After they filed out, he asked Suman, "What didn't you want to say in front of them?"

"You learned the Dangers of the Raven along with the Dangers and Advantages of every other House. Did you never think to apply them to Kayin?"

Anari's throat constricted. He had to swallow several times before he could speak. "You believe Kayin is behind this."

"I doubt he is the only one. Testing the other heirs is a normal part of the succession struggle. The oba must have a strong connection to the gods, or the whole country will suffer. Better that we know which heirs don't receive divine protection before the final challenge."

"Like me. Better that I'm eliminated," Anari said bitterly.

For once, Suman didn't scold him to guard his tongue. He didn't disagree, either. "We know Kayin was behind at least one attempt."

"Which one? How do you know?"

"What House did you think the man who poisoned you belonged to?"

"House Crow."

"Why?"

"He had the dark eyes and hair of House Crow. His right hand had been amputated, so there was no House mark to prove otherwise."

"What generation of House Crow traits did he have?"

Anari hated the way that Suman dropped back into his old habit of making an argument by asking a series of questions. He hadn't liked it when Suman was still his teacher, and he didn't like it now. He especially didn't like the inevitable destination of the questions.

"An older generation. My mother's, or perhaps the one before that."

"How are the older generations different?"

They look like House Raven. Instead of answering the question, Anari argued against the conclusion. "He could belong to a different House. House Rat, maybe, or House Viper. House Horse, if he is a gray who dyes his hair."

Suman opened his mouth, but Anari continued to speak. "Except he showed none of the traits of those other Houses. And I already said why he can't be Scorned."

Suman nodded.

"Which leaves House Raven and Kayin." Anari

shook his head. "It doesn't make sense, though. Kayin never lusted after the oba's beaded crown. He believed he should not rule."

As children, neither Anari nor Kayin had aspired to be crowned oba after their seed-father. When Anari began following Kayin around and imitating the older boy, Adetosoye could have ended it and sent Anari back to his House in disgrace. Instead, he'd accepted Anari as an heir equal to Kayin and in need of the same guidance. At the time, the two were as equal in their chances of achieving the crown as they were in their lack of desire for it.

One day, Adetosoye had found them arguing over how to discourage one of the semi-tame courtyard monkeys from stealing the smooth, round rocks they collected to practice flinging with their slings.

Kayin held his sling in his left hand and one of the few unpurloined rocks in his right.

Anari was wrapped around Kayin's sling arm. "No!" he yelled. "Talk to the guard first!"

"I can take care of it!" Kayin shouted. He tried to shake Anari off his arm, but Anari clung tight.

"What is the cause of this?" Adetosoye's deep voice boomed behind them.

The sound startled Anari into loosening his grip. Kayin yanked his arm free.

"One of the monkeys stole our rocks," Kayin said shortly. "I was going to take care of it, but he won't let me!"

"That's not the right way to fix it!" Kayin protested.

Adetosoye sighed. "I knew this day would come, but I did not expect it to be today. Come sit beside me."

He sat on one of the courtyard's wooden benches.

Kayin sat on one side of him. Anari leaned against the other.

"If one of you becomes oba, you will have to confront many problems during your reign. Anari, what will you do when there is trouble?"

As Adetosoye spoke, Anari felt the reverberations of his words where he leaned against him.

"Gather my allies and advisors," Anari said promptly. "We will mob together and attack the problem until we solve it."

"And you, Kayin?"

"I will hunt down the cause of the trouble. I will target it in everything I do, and I will do anything to destroy it."

"That is one of the differences between House Crow and House Raven," Adetosoye said.

Anari pulled away from Adetosoye. His shoulders slumped and he stared at his feet. "You think I would make the wrong decision."

Adetosoye's deep voice was gentle as he answered. "You are in House Raven's courtyard, but you do not belong to Lord Raven. You are of Lord Crow's flock. I think you would make a *different* decision."

"I told him—"

Adetosoye raised one large hand. Kayin cut his speech off.

"You are both royal heirs. No matter how you do it, you know your first responsibility is to protect our people. In that you are the same. Yes?"

Neither boy answered.

"Yes?" Adetosoye nudged them.

"Yes," Anari mumbled.

"Yes," Kayin said grudgingly.

"Good. No more fighting about this." He wrapped

his arms around both boys and gave them a quick shoulder hug.

They hadn't fought about it again, Anari remembered. The larcenous monkey had disappeared not long afterward, and the thefts had stopped with him.

That event held a new and terrible meaning for Anari after his own poisoning.

"If Kayin has decided that he must be oba, he won't stop until he's destroyed even the slightest threat," Anari told Suman.

"We need a strong oba," his protocol advisor replied. "Kayin could be one."

A chill went through Anari. "He'll try to kill me again. This time he won't risk a gradual death. But why? What could make him do this?"

"We are throwing our warriors onto the battlefield like wood on a funeral pyre. If we lose, our country is what will burn." Suman's voice deepened. "Men will do anything to save their home. Never forget that."

Anari shook his head, but he didn't argue. Suman's words caught his attention. They suggested a solution. *Like wood on a funeral pyre ...* and who noticed one log among others when there was a corpse on the pyre? Nobody would expect him to run *toward* danger to save his   life.

4

"I DON'T LIKE this," the head of the household guard said bluntly. "I can't protect you on the battlefield."

"I won't be on the battlefield," Anari said, answering the worry in his mother's eyes as much as the guard's protest. "I'll be with the Crow chief healer, surrounded by our people and hidden among them. Who can pick out one crow from a flock? As long as I cover the royal birthmark on my chest and the absence of a tattoo on my hand, I will simply be one more wounded Crow." He raised his bandaged right hand in illustration.

"You could do the same here. Pretend to be an ordinary member of our House recovering from a war wound."

"I can't hide in Ayeli Asatsvyi, even among the flock. Everybody knows that only the royal heirs have no House tattoo. Aside from the Scorned, of course."

"You would have to travel. That puts you in danger," Anari's mother protested.

"Romesh," Anari prompted.

"The Eye of House Crow asked me if I could smuggle him to the battlefront in a shipment of healing supplies," Romesh said. "I can. Once he's inside the healer's tent, he will be one among many. Nobody but Crows will see him. Even they will not mark his presence. But he will be surrounded by warriors ready to defend him if he is revealed. He is right. It is the best option."

"I still don't like it," growled the head of the household guard. "Too much can go wrong. It's a battlefield. You have no idea how chaotic it is."

"I have heard your concerns," Anari told him.

The guard bowed his head. He didn't give voice to any of the other protests that were clearly running through his mind.

After that, it all happened very fast. Anari had come up with the plan and given the order, but part of him still expected something to halt it. Romesh emptied out a large crate and padded it with quilts. Anari's mother left briefly. When she returned, she carried a small embroidered purse.

"Here," she said. "The guard was right, you know. If there's one thing my life has taught me, it's that you can't predict your future. You can only try to prepare."

Anari opened up the purse and saw the silver glint of rupiya coins and the gleam of brass bits. "I won't need this."

She tilted her head in a shrug. "It's only money."

Anari slid the purse into his pocket and wrapped his mother in an embrace. His chin rested on top of her head. For a moment, he wished he was still young enough to throw his arms around her waist and believe that she could be his shield against the world, but time could not run backward. It was his duty to protect her.

The best way he could do that at the moment was to leave and lead the danger away.

"This will help to control the pain," Romesh said, holding out a bowl half-filled with liquid.

Anari broke the embrace and faced his future. The preparation tasted like cinnamon and licorice, and it burned on its way down. He shuddered once after he swallowed it.

He settled into the most comfortable position he could find inside the crate. Romesh and the head guard set the lid in place. Anari flinched at the first sharp crack of the hammer sealing him in. After that, he held still. Crows hated traps, but this was his idea.

They summoned porters to carry the crate out to the waiting cart, packed Romesh's other healing supplies around it, and then the cart was underway and it was too late for Anari to change his mind.

Through narrow cracks between the crate slats, he watched farmers tending their fields, merchants chivying along their caravans, and children playing a game of Eight Houses in the dust of the road. He sipped sparingly from his water jug and nibbled at fried lentil balls.

As the day wore on, the heat inside the crate increased until Anari finally fell into a feverish half-sleep.

"Where's the Crow chief healer?"

The question jolted Anari fully awake.

"At the edge of the battlefield, but the infidels are pushing us hard. He might need to relocate farther behind the line. Ask him before you unload."

"Yes, sir," said the cart driver. He didn't sound enthusiastic. The cart resumed bouncing over the rough terrain.

Anari heard a thud beside his head and pulled back to see the sharp point of an arrow sticking through the crate. The cart horse screamed, and the cart lurched forward. Anari's head smacked against the side of the crate, driving nails of pain into the base of his skull. He groaned. The runaway cart rattled across the battlefield at alarming speed. Anari was tossed around inside his crate like a sack of laundry. By the time the cart overbalanced, he didn't know which way was up.

The slats cracked when the crate hit the ground. Anari kicked one side again and again until he made a hole big enough to crawl through. He pushed himself to his feet, only to nearly lose his head as a war club whistled past him and crushed the skull of an infidel warrior.

"Sacred Hyena!" swore the warrior who'd thrown the weapon. "I almost killed you. Find a weapon before someone else does more than *almost*, and get to your wing." He marched off, stopping now and then to bring his war club down to finish off a wounded infidel.

The supply cart lay overturned behind Anari. Still in its traces, the cart horse thrashed on the ground. An arrow jutted from its throat. Blood poured from the wound. Its legs churned the red-brown mud.

Anari glanced around. He stood on a ravaged battlefield in the center of a temporary lull in the fighting. The dubious safety of the Eight Houses camps lay far behind him, beside a grove of trees that hugged the river. Anari could see that once this had been a prosperous farm, but the grain was trampled into the ground, and the mud brick walls of the farmers' home had caved in.

Ahead of him, a mob of infidel warriors hacked at the defenders of a halted war chariot that had broken through their line, leaving a swathe of dead and wounded in its wake. To either side, fierce knots of fighting swirled along the wings of the battle. The wings were swinging back as the infidels pushed forward. Warriors fought over the bodies of their fallen brethren. The air was thick with the scent of blood, sweat, and the offal reek of death. Crows dared the edges of the battlefield, and ravens circled above the area where the fighting was the thickest.

Anari frowned. What he saw did not make sense. The infidels fought with as much desperation as the warriors of the Eight Houses. Though the infidels were outnumbered, they did not retreat. They were the invaders, but they fought as though it were for their last chance at life.

He felt an urge to ask them what could possibly matter that much.

"Forgive me, Lord Crow!" he prayed out loud, horrified that he'd considered something so blasphemous. His only comfort was the thin justification that from the moment the oba had returned to House Fox, the royal heirs were given a holy exemption from the edicts against contamination by those outside the Eight Houses.

The wail of pipes came from behind the line held by the infidels. Anari squinted and saw their warriors gathering together. They would charge. The wings of the Eight Houses battle formation would sweep back, the fight would shift, and he was about to be engulfed in the thick of it.

Unarmed and unarmored, he stood little chance of survival. It had taken him only a few moments to assess the battlefield. He could still catch the Hyena warrior before the fighting reached them.

Anari hurried after him. House Hyena had announced that they would not pursue the beaded crown. Anari would be relatively safe in the Hyena warrior's custody.

As he approached, however, a giant infidel who had broken through the battle line finished his opponent and glanced around for another. When he saw the Hyena warrior, an expression of anticipation crossed his sun-burnished face and he strode forward to meet him. The Hyena warrior hurled his war club at the infidel's skull. The infidel dodged with startling speed for one so large. His lips pulled back from his teeth in something that was part snarl and part triumphant smile.

Anari dropped to one knee. He knew the way to call on Lord Crow's war blessing. It was the only way he might be able to help the Hyena warrior. Lord Crow had never granted Anari that blessing, but Anari had never sought it in true desperation. If ever Lord Crow would respond, it would be now.

Anari screamed the harsh cry of a crow. He curved his arms out like wings and rose, keeping his back bent.

The Hyena warrior drew his thin, curved sword. The infidel slashed at the warrior. The warrior blocked the strike barely in time. Their sword hilts locked as they strained to push each other off-balance.

Anari stomped in a circle, raising and lowering his arms to gather Lord Crow's blessing. He didn't feel any different.

The Hyena warrior was brave and strong, but he was losing. He knew it. He pushed away from the infidel, leaping backwards and lowering his sword to strike at the infidel's forearms. Had the infidel been as slow as he was large, it would have worked.

Instead, the infidel twisted to the side and rolled his wrists to bring his sword blurring across in a horizontal stroke that slammed into the warrior's armored side.

Anari raised his arm and slashed it down in a gesture that should have knocked the infidel back. Nothing happened.

The force of the infidel's blow made the hyena warrior grunt and nearly drop his sword. Too close to use his own weapon, the infidel slammed his elbow hard against the warrior's jaw. The warrior staggered back a step. The infidel raised his sword high and swung it in an arc that ended with a spurt of blood and an eerie whistling sound as the hyena warrior fell to the ground.

The infidel took a step forward, and Anari saw his own death coming. He cast a quick glance around him. A broken spear lay a few feet away. He stooped and seized it.

He would fight, but he didn't delude himself that he had a chance. He settled into a defensive stance, fixed the Virtues of the Crow in his mind, and prepared himself for what would follow.

He was reciting the Second Virtue of the Crow: Collecting the Precious when his life was spared.

An arrow punctured the infidel's eye and lodged deep inside his head. The infidel raised one hand, as if he were going to pull it out and keep fighting. Then he toppled over and did not move again.

"—and to pluck value from what others discard without thought," Anari continued. The recitation helped him to keep his hands from shaking.

Ravens swirled through the sky above the battlefield. The churn of combat would soon reach him.

"The Fifth Virtue of the Crow: Choosing One's Battle. Observe the crow. He does not rush into danger without his kin by his side. If he is alone, he will hide from an intruder until he can gather his kin to mob and destroy the enemy. Pointless defeat is avoided, and victory is certain and overwhelming. This is the wisdom of the crow," he continued automatically.

He blinked. He faced an enemy that vastly outnumbered him. That was not the Crow way. He looked around. The trees were too far away for him to reach, the collapsed house provided little shelter, and the broken cart was too exposed. His gaze moved reluctantly to the dead.

Crows did not disdain to use any tool that came to hand. That didn't help settle his stomach, but it did steel his resolve. He stripped off his overrobe, dipped it in the blood that had spilled from the Hyena warrior, and pulled it back on. The blood instantly soaked through his robe and oozed down his back. If his body were exposed, he had to blend in. Nobody would believe Anari was dead if his body looked untouched. Hopefully, the precaution would be unnecessary because nobody would see him.

He knelt next to the largest pile of corpses, one where four had fallen together, and crawled between them. He took shallow breaths through his mouth, but the stench of meat just beginning to go off wormed its way inside his nostrils. He swallowed down an upsurge of bile. He had expected corpses to be stiff, but lying in the heat for hours had made them soft and squishy. They could not be mistaken for living flesh.

One of the corpses sighed against his cheek like a lover. The fine hairs on the back of his neck stood on end. He knew dead bodies released gases, but the theoretical knowledge hadn't prepared him.

He was almost completely hidden, but he couldn't bear to bury his face. He thought he would go mad if he were trapped in the damp and rotting darkness beneath the corpses. A group of ravens flew overhead. Anari rested his head on the amputated arm of a dead warrior and remembered when he'd learned the differences between crows and ravens.

5

Twelve years ago.

ANARI BEGAN SEEKING out Kayin when Anari was ten and Kayin was thirteen. He trailed after him so much that the servants of House Raven called Anari "the crow that would be a raven." They laughed after they said that, but Anari didn't understand why. To him, crows and ravens were the same thing: big, black, clever birds. The Keeper of the Crows had introduced him to the household crows, and they looked much the same as the carved wooden sculpture of ravens in Kayin's room. So he did what he'd always done when he was confused: he asked Kayin.

Kayin's lips pressed tight and his shoulders swelled. For the first time, Anari felt afraid of the older boy he idolized.

"I am of House Raven and you are of House Crow," Kayin explained. "What they meant was that you wanted to join House Raven. That's a cruel thing for them to say. I will see to it that they do not call you by that nickname again. It's not your fault that you weren't born to House Raven. Before Lord Crow had enough believers to form a new eighth House, Band Crow was part of House Raven. If you'd been born in the time of our great-great-grandparents, you would have been a member of House Raven. Now, though, a Crow cannot become a Raven any more than a Horse could become a Hyena."

The note of disdain in Kayin's voice made Anari want to hide. He lowered his eyes and stuffed his hands in the pockets of his robe. Kayin noticed his reaction. He sighed and patted Anari's head.

"It's not your fault. When you're older, you'll learn the Temptations and Virtues of the Crow," Kayin told him. "You'll understand better then. For now, just remember that crows and ravens are very different. Ravens are much larger. Ravens like to soar high above the ground so they can see everything at once, while crows like to stay below the treetops, so they are protected from predators. Ravens—"

Anari listened. He cheered up, bit by bit. He enjoyed learning about the totems of the Houses. Unfortunately, Kayin chose to end the lesson with an example that would give Anari nightmares for weeks.

"Crows like to flock. Together, they make a murder of crows. A group of ravens, called an unkindness, only comes together in two places: battlefields and graveyards, where the bones of men fall."

Anari stared up at Kayin. He seemed to be amused by this little fact, but it made Anari's stomach queasy.

Kayin ruffled Anari's hair. "You'd better run home to your mother. You know how she worries."

Anari nodded solemnly. He knew his mother only allowed him to visit Kayin because she had no living brother to act as his guide-father, and Adetosoye had taken on part of that responsibility.

"Did she make you promise not to eat any bean cakes that my mother gave you?"

Anari nodded again.

Kayin sighed. "Go on, brat," he said.

As Anari closed the door to House Raven's wing in the royal palace, he heard Kayin mutter, "As if a Raven royal wife would stoop to robbing a Crow's nest."

6

Now.

THE AIR OF the battlefield rang with the metallic shriek of clashing swords, the harsh breath of fighters, and the groans and sobs of the dying. Feet tromped past Anari's hiding place, but nobody inspected it closely enough to determine that one of the bodies was only pretending to be dead. Once, a warrior fell so close that his outstretched arm nearly brushed Anari's face. The squirrel tattoo on his hand marked him as being born to Band Squirrel in House Rat. Anari sent up a brief prayer that the warrior's god would find him worthy.

Anari would have sworn that it was impossible to fall asleep in the middle of a battle, but the clash of swords sounded more and more like the music of the shining silver chimes that had lulled him to sleep for years. Romesh's preparation must still be affecting him, he thought drowsily. His eyes drifted shut.

He woke screaming. Agony radiated from his right eye. Spikes of pain drove into his cheek. His muscles thrummed and his bones vibrated in sympathetic torment. It felt as though molten lead were being poured over his head.

He kept screaming and flung his arm up in front of his face. A loud caw next to his ear deafened him. The spikes were wrenched from his cheek. Feathers brushed against his hand.

He could see with his left eye, but not his right. Twilight spread across the battlefield. The warriors were pulling back to their camps before it grew too dark to tell friend from foe. He reached up and touched his eye. His world splintered into shards of pain that fell into unconsciousness.

When he swam up to awareness again, the entire right half of his face was hot and swollen. His throat felt raw, as if he'd continued screaming in his sleep. He could not open his right eye.

Night's curtain had fallen fully. The only light came from a sliver of moon and the twinkle of stars moving across the sky and the battlefield.

Anari shook his head groggily. Stars didn't move across the ground. He stared at the column of lights crossing the battlefield. All he could see were dark figures.

His sight was limited; very well, he would use the other tools he had.

He quieted his breathing as much as he could and strove to pick out any noise not native to the battlefield. At first, all he heard were the groans of the dying, the snarls of feral dogs warning each other away from their chosen carrion, and a rhythmic *tock-tock* like the tapping of a speckle-breasted woodpecker. He focused past those sounds. At the very edge of his hearing, he made out a low muttering. Try as he might, he could not understand the words. The other noises on the battlefield interfered too much.

Though it was the last thing he wished to do, he inhaled deeply. He smelled blood, piss, and excrement mixed with putrefaction and rot. His stomach roiled, and acid vomit burned its way up his throat. He swallowed hard, waited a moment, and tried again. This time he noticed a smoky scent underlying the stench of battle.

The smoke, the lights, and the strange sounds came together to paint a clear picture in Anari's mind. Lord Raven's priests were on the battlefield.

The snaking column of lights was composed of Lord Raven's priests. What was on a battlefield was theirs. As their chant consoled the spirit of the dead, they positioned a spike above the corpse's forehead and cracked open the skull with two swift blows of their hammer. *Tock-tock*, and the spirit was released from the body. The smoke from their censers took the place of the cremation pyre and showed the spirit the way back to the god of their House.

The priests would kill Anari without hesitation when they discovered who he was. Inside the city walls, bound under the laws decreed by the Eight Houses, they would not move openly against the heir of another House. Only the royal heirs were given that freedom, and only during the succession struggle. Even then, the heirs were expected to use their personal resources and whatever blessings the favor of their god had granted them. On the battlefield, the Raven priests labored under no such compunctions.

Shortly after they saw the royal birthmark on Anari's chest, there would be one less contender against the Raven royal heir.

Anari tried to shove the corpses off of him and knew a minute of sheer panic when they refused to budge. The warrior on top of him leered through a mouth of broken teeth. Anari forced himself to relax and move slowly. Brute strength was not the answer.

It felt as if it took forever. Every time anything brushed the right side of his face, waves of pain threatened to overwhelm him.

The world wavered uncertainly around him when he stood. The priests had no reason to venture among the trees on the far side of the battlefield. All he had to do was make it there.

His face burned with fever heat. Whenever he blinked his one good eye, the ground shifted beneath his feet. He shuffled forward with tentative half steps, moving as gingerly as an old man bent over his cane.

In that way, he made it across three-quarters of the battlefield before he fell.

The Raven priests were close. The smoke from their incense shrouded the battlefield, and their lanterns had swelled too large to be mistaken for distant stars. Their chanting filled the air.

The mere thought of standing exhausted Anari. He pushed himself up until he was on hands and knees, his head hanging down. He crawled toward the trees.

He imagined that the dead warriors he crawled over were talking to him. Some cheered him on. Some urged him to give in to the inevitable. The infidel dead just mocked him. Anari was composing a scathing rebuttal to an accusation of cowardice when he realized that his audience was behind him. The lumps he crawled over were tree roots, not bodies. The glimmer of light far ahead of him was the moon on the water, not the lanterns of the priests. The air that he breathed smelled of loam and leaves, not death. The rhythmic chanting that he heard was the song of crickets. He had made it to the forest's edge. He forced himself to crawl another two yards before collapsing.

He dreamed.

A huge raven battered its wings against the window, its beak open in a harsh battle cry. Anari stumbled backwards and fell to the floor. Rats poured from the corners of the room. They began to bite him. He tried to bat them away, but there were too many. They were everywhere, biting at his legs and hands and face. The light in the room brightened. It scared the rats away, but it kept getting brighter and hotter. His face was on fire. He whimpered and tried to hide from the sun by digging into the ground.

"Here," squeaked the voice of a rat, "there's a man here. He's alive, but he's hurt pretty badly. I think he's feverish."

He heard the rustle of skirts as the rat knelt beside him. He tried to open his eyes, but the effort shot a spear of pain through his face. He passed out.

He woke from a dream of the rocking horse that he had ridden as a child. The bed he was in kept swinging back and forth. Something warm and wet covered his eyes. An argument was being conducted in hissed whispers beside his bed.

"—don't know what I was thinking of, girl, to let you bring him aboard. For all we know, he could be one of the infidels!"

The owner of the deep, rough voice sounded irritated.

"Captain! He's dressed like city folk. He isn't an infidel." The girl's voice ladled ridicule on the very idea.

"Then he's a Scorned one, because he sure doesn't

have a Band tattoo on his hand. I didn't bargain on
taking another Scorned aboard. Might cause me trouble
with the port overseer. He'll overlook a little help,
knowing as how I can't afford a proper crew from the
Bands, but if I've got two of you, he'll think I'm trying
to dodge paying what's right."

"Anyone with eyes—" She stopped abruptly, and
Anari wondered why. "Anyone can see that he's not fit
for work."

"And that's another thing! He's lying here in my
cabin, taking up the time of my crew. I can't afford that.
Why did I let you bring him aboard?"

"You must have taken leave of your senses," she
said dryly, "and forgotten for a moment that you don't
have an ounce of kindness or charity in you. If you're
so worried about the cost, I'll work this run for free."

There was a grumbling noise, like the complaint of
a bear roused early from hibernation. Anari grinned at
the notion of a bear as captain. He imagined a bear
standing on his hind legs, with one paw on the ship's
wheel.

The girl gasped. "He smiled! Do you think he's
coming around?"

A hand touched his arm. "Can you tell us your
name? What happened to you?"

Anari would have answered, but his tongue was too
heavy and their voices kept sliding farther into the
distance.

When Anari woke up again, he knew that he had
been dreaming. He was on a ship—he could feel it rise
and fall and hear the slap of waves against the hull—
but he doubted it was captained by a bear. He lay in a
swaying rope hammock. Sweat drenched his body. A
wet cloth covered his right eye.

He raised his arm. The effort it took shocked him. The bandage he'd wrapped around his hand was gone, baring the smooth, unmarked skin on the back of his hand to the world. At least he was still in the same clothes he had worn on the battlefield, crusted in blood though they were. He doubted that his unexpected rescuers had seen the royal birthmark on his chest.

He hesitated and then lifted the wet cloth from his right eye. His eye throbbed, and he couldn't see out of it. An astringent herbal smell rose from the cloth. He tangled his fingers in the hammock rope and pulled himself up, though the simple motion exhausted him. He turned his head to survey the room with his left eye.

He saw a small, bare room. He assumed it was below deck, because there was neither window nor porthole to let light in, only a lit lamp fixed to the wall. A mirror was bolted to the wall beside the lamp. Anari knew that as soon as he gathered the strength to stand, he would have to confront his reflection. A basin holding soiled rags sat beside the door. He glanced at the wet cloth that had covered his eyes and, to his horror, saw bloodstains.

A rustling noise to his right made him jerk his head around and crane his neck. He felt horribly vulnerable. Anyone could sneak up on his right side, and he would never know it. Anyone at—

The thought vanished when he saw what was beside him. For a moment, he forgot to breathe. On top of a bolted-down trunk to Anari's right crouched a man the size of a ten-year-old, watching him intently. His skin was the black of a starless night, and his hair gleamed blue-black in the lamplight. His eyes were shining black orbs with no white around their edges. Seeing that Anari was looking at him, the man cocked his head so far to the side that Anari felt dizzy.

"Lord Crow!" Anari gasped.

"Humph," the god said. "You do look like carrion."

He straightened his head and gave a quick shake of his shoulders that made his skin ripple, except it wasn't skin. The dim light had misled Anari. Thousands of tiny black feathers covered Lord Crow. Only his face, hands, and feet were bare.

Anari would have flung himself to grovel on the floor, but Lord Crow put a hand on his shoulder to stop him. Anari's skin shuddered under the touch of his god, but he stayed in the hammock.

"No, you definitely have too much life in you to be carrion," Lord Crow said, sounding irritated. "One of mine wronged you; crows should not feed upon the living. It is twice the offense since my wing also extends over you. The crow who took your eye has been punished, but I still owe you a favor."

Thoughts flapped through Anari's mind, but he could catch none of them. "What—?"

"No wishing for immortal life or anything of that sort, mind you," Lord Crow warned him. "I couldn't even use trickery to give you a semblance of that. It must be a favor that is within my domain to grant."

The shadows cast by the single lamp played tricks with Anari's sight, so that Lord Crow seemed to shift between being very close and very far away. Anari's head throbbed, and he closed his eyes for a moment.

"Not that I would deny or trick someone out of a rightful claim," Lord Crow said in a huffy tone, as if Anari's silence accused him of just that, "no more than I would push a chick into the air before its wings fledged. That is not the way of the crow."

Lord Crow plucked a feather from his shoulder and pressed his hand against Anari's chest, on top of the birthmark that proved Anari's claim of being the Crow royal heir. Anari felt a sharp pain, as though his skin had been pierced with an arrow, though the god's hand was only resting on top of his robe. Lord Crow cocked his head to survey Anari again.

He nodded. "It is done. When you are ready to claim your favor, call for me."

"What—?" Anari began to ask.

Shadows spread from Lord Crow's shoulders like wings. The sight dizzied Anari, and he had to close his eyes again. He heard the deafening flap of huge wings. He felt an impossible wind blow through the cabin. When he opened his eyes, Lord Crow was gone.

Anari unfastened his robe and stared at his birthmark. A shadowy blemish lay beneath one wing of the crow. He pressed his hand over it. Something fluttered against his palm, and he jerked his hand away.

"Come back!" he shouted to the empty air.

Lord Crow did not answer, but Anari heard the rapid patter of feet running in his direction. He clutched his robe closed and began buttoning it just as the door was flung open.

A girl hurtled into the room. She looked about thirteen, much younger than regular ship's crew. Sailing Bands only signed their children to apprentice on a ship after the age of fourteen, but she moved across the cabin with the ease of long experience. As she passed the lamp, he saw that she had a red tint to her brown hair that spoke of House Fox. When she reached his bedside, he noticed that her hands had the long, delicate fingers of House Rat.

He glanced at the back of her hand. All became

clear. It lacked the tattoo showing her Band. She was a Scorned one, one of those not sanctioned by the gods of the Eight Houses.

"You're awake!" she said.

Anari recognized her voice from his fever dreams. She was the rat who had saved him, except she was no Rat at all. Gratitude warred with outrage. He could have died in the forest without her. If not at the hands of the Raven priests, then from wound fever.

Yet his entire being recoiled from owing a debt to a Scorned one. They existed, yes, but they were to be shunned. They were beggars and dung collectors. They were a blight upon the gods'-ordained order of the world. They were not to be traded with, not to be touched, not to be spoken to. They were those who had been refused by the gods, and the god-fearing obeyed that stricture or became Scorned themselves.

Before the war, border priests collected infidel goods left at the border, ritually cleansed them, and left unwanted surplus for the infidels in exchange. Even the priests never spoke to or traded directly with the infidels, who were unquestionably Scorned because they had been born outside of the Eight Houses.

That a Scorned one worked as crew aboard a ship was an affront to the gods. They could send the vessel to the bottom of the river at any moment.

Anari averted his eyes and waited for her to leave. The Scorned knew their place. She would take the hint.

Incredibly, she kept talking. "My name is Rasee," she said, standing with her hands on her hips. "How does your—your eye feel?"

The hesitation made his gut twist. He needed to know the worst.

"I wonder if the captain will be down soon to help

me look in the mirror," he said, addressing the air in front of him.

"We don't need him!" she said. "I'm lots stronger than I look, and you're not so big."

When she walked toward the hammock, he realized with shock that she was going to touch him. He tried to move away, fighting the hammock to get up and out before she reached him. His arms shook. His fingers trembled. His joints throbbed with agony.

"Is it your eye?" Rasee asked, hurrying forward.

"Don't touch me!" he gasped. He pushed himself away from her, but his arms gave out and he collapsed back into the hammock.

"You're the one that stinks," she said. "What are you putting on airs for? You're no better than I am!"

She dared to compare him to herself! Anari opened his mouth to put her in her place, angry enough to address her directly and take the penalties ... and stopped, mouth half-open.

He could not tell anyone who he really was. A chill crept over him as he realized the full import of what that meant. The only people without a Band tattoo were the royal heirs—and the Scorned. He must pretend to be one of them.

At least he had a holy exemption from the rules forbidding contact with the Scorned. This would not pollute him. It only felt like it.

"I'm sorry," he said. The clamor of "Sacrilege!" still rang through his mind. "I'm confused. From the fever."

She accepted his weak excuse. Her smile returned. "Are you sure you want to look in the mirror?" she asked. "It's pretty bad."

He nodded.

She helped him out of the hammock. His skin crawled under her touch.

"Scared?" she asked.

He would have been angry, but her tone suggested nothing but empathy. For a heartbeat, he wondered what this girl had suffered in her life as a Scorned one.

No. If he were to succeed in this heretical charade, he must avoid thinking of her as a Scorned one. She'd said her name was Rasee. He would be helped by Rasee, not "a Scorned one." He would lean on *Rasee's* shoulder. *Rasee* would support him while he confronted his reflection.

He silently repeated her name as a mantra while she led him to the mirror. He would have fallen more than once without the help of—without Rasee's help, he admitted.

Then he faced the mirror, and all thoughts of heresies and abominations fled.

He stared into a nightmare. Scabbed-over gouges pockmarked his right cheek deeply enough to scar him for life, and that was the least of it. The center of his right eye was gone, as if it had been scooped out. The wound wept a blood-tinted clear fluid. The white of the eye looked sunken, like a slowly draining water flask. Anari guessed that in time, what was left of his eye would be a dry, shriveled, leathery thing. He had seen beggars with similar deformities. Now, he felt that same horrified pity when he looked at his reflection.

The lingering effects of the poison still wracked his body, but he could endure them until the cascade restored the power of the healer priests. After that, Romesh would heal him and it would be as if the poisoning had never happened.

His eye would still be gone. Not even the most

powerful healer priest could grow a new body part.

Rasee waited silently until Anari turned his face away from his reflection. She helped him back to the hammock. She handed him a fresh compress for his eye and a clean, worn robe that had obviously been sized to fit the captain. Then she left without a word, an unexpected kindness. He listened to the sounds of her and the captain moving the ship's cargo out onto the pier as he thought. They were not pleasant thoughts. He had no idea where to go. He daren't approach his family or any of the Crow temples; they would be watched.

He had only himself to rely on. No. He had less than himself. His hand lifted toward his face and stopped. As House heir, he had resources. As an unmarked cripple, he had nothing.

He could demand that Lord Crow repair his eye. He placed his hand on top of his royal birthmark and felt the wing flutter eagerly under his palm. The favor wanted to be used. But if he used it now to heal himself, then what? He would still be in the same straits. Besides which, a favor from Lord Crow was not to be used without proper forethought. The Crow god was a trickster. It would be in his nature to take a simple wish and twist it into something far from what the requester had intended.

Anari thought of that hot season afternoon when he and Kayin had sparred for the last time. It had taught him that healing one wound sometimes inflicted another. He would have only one chance at this. It was worth waiting to be certain that what he asked for was worth the price.

The thump and scrape of Rasee and the captain moving their cargo onto the pier eventually stopped. A little later, Rasee returned to the cabin where Anari lay.

She carried a heavy stick in one hand.

"Here," she said, handing it to Anari, "this will do to support you until the fever's weakness has passed."

"What time is it?" he asked.

"Sunset," she told him. "I found you this morning, and you were feverish all day while we sailed to Alhadd."

He calculated. He'd spent a night on the battlefield. He only had to survive for three more days. After that, a new oba would be crowned. Then Anari could safely go into exile with a small household and the resources to support them. If he left before, he would be on his own and truly Scorned.

He patted his pocket and felt the reassuring weight of the purse. He had enough to rent a room for three days. He could order food and have them leave it outside his door. One look at his eye and they would believe his claim of sickness.

"I need a bandage for my hand," he told her.

Her eyes widened. "What are you planning to do?"

"Don't worry," he reassured her. "I simply need to keep my hand covered for a few days."

She shook her head vigorously. "That gets people killed. You might think you can mix with *them*, but you can't."

He reminded himself that such irrational fear was to be expected from the Scorned.

"Thank you for treating my eye," he said. He hesitated and then pulled a rupiya out of his purse. "This is for you, in exchange for your help."

She gave him a long look. "You haven't been on your own long, have you?"

"What do you mean?" Anari demanded. He prepared to muffle her in case she tried to announce his true identity to the world.

"They kept you," she said, her eyes shining with wonder. "Your family kept you. They hid you as long as they could."

"Don't speak of my family," he warned her. As if the royal Crow household would ever shelter a Scorned one.

She didn't appear cowed by the rebuke, if she even recognized it as such. "You'll be needing that coin more than I will. At least I know how to stay out of trouble. You come with me and maybe you'll learn, but you should still save that until you need it."

He bridled at her refusal. He had offered her good money—had even lowered himself to phrase it as a trade!—and she had turned him down. Who did she think she was?

No, he reminded himself. Who did she think *he* was?

"I've got a place you can stay," she continued.

He wanted to shudder at the idea of living with the Scorned, but he forced himself to smile and nod. She meant it as a kindness. He could treat it as such, even if he had no intention of going with her.

"I do not need to come with you," he assured her. "I have sufficient funds to rent a room."

She gave him a look that he couldn't interpret. "Have you now? Well, I'll just see you to your room to be certain."

The captain did not wish them farewell when they left. For all the attention he paid to them, they might have been a pair of mice scuttling across the dock.

Rasee let Anari take the lead as they went into the city. She didn't try to strike up further conversation, for which he was glad. He did wish that she would stop watching him with that odd gleam in her eye, though. It reminded him of one of the Dangers of the Fox: The Lure. Beware following the fox, for he will slip around the side of a pit, leaving you to fall into it. He shrugged the feeling off. She was Scorned; the teachings of the Eight Houses did not apply.

Anari had never been to the docks, but he reasoned that there must be hostels nearby with rooms to rent. When a pair of servants hurried by with baskets of fresh fish for their household's cook, Anari stepped forward. Rasee gasped, but he ignored her.

"Excuse me," he began, "could you direct me to—"

The woman hissed through her teeth and drew back. The man shoved Anari away with the basket of fish that he carried. Anari stumbled and fell to one knee. The servants hurried away without a backward glance.

"What is wrong with you?" Rasee demanded as she offered her arm and braced for him to pull himself up.

"I was only asking—"

"You fool! You're lucky that they were in a hurry. Usually, you'd get beaten for trying that."

Anari began to worry about the practicality of renting a room, but he could hardly stay with Rasee and her kind. She seemed a decent girl, for a Scorned one, but it was still wrong.

"The guards will be out soon to make sure there's no troublemakers about," Rasee said. When Anari didn't respond, she added, "So you know, that's us."

He was relieved to round a corner and see a freshly painted sign advertising food and lodgings. In the bottom right corner of the sign, a rat nibbled on a groundnut. A member of House Rat must be the owner of the hostel. It was a common occupation for the gregarious Rats.

"No need to worry about that now," he said, striding up to the door.

He'd worked out a plan to rent a room without causing offense to the owner, but he wasn't surprised to see Rasee hang back, unwilling to enter.

"You can wait here," he told her kindly. Drawing attention to the misfortunes of others was not the Crow way. It was not her fault that she had no Virtues to guide her in the ways of courage and right behavior.

"I'll do that," she told him.

He was pleased to find the hostel's dining hall mostly empty when he stepped inside. He walked past the burly door guard with his chin up as if he had a perfect right to be there. A plump, pink-cheeked man with the large ears of House Rat bustled up, smiling.

"Welcome! I am Musa of Band Squirrel, House Rat, the proprietor of this hostel." He reached for the traditional handclasp.

Anari kept his hands in his pockets.

Musa's smile turned to a scowl.

"What a nice establishment," Anari said very quietly. He did not speak directly to the proprietor, though he knew Musa's sensitive ears would be able to hear him. "I'm sure a person would enjoy staying here for three days. Why, they would never want to leave their room!"

Musa's eyebrows climbed up his forehead.

It was not the reaction Anari had hoped for. He plowed on.

"Though I'm sure the prices are quite high for such fine lodgings." He hefted the embroidered purse in his pocket. The coins clinked against each other.

That was a mistake. His voice might not have carried, but the sound of money surely did. The other guests glanced in their direction.

Musa looked irritated. His voice was loud as he proclaimed to the room, "Scorned ones are not welcome here! This is a respectable place!"

The guests nodded approvingly and leaned back as if to watch a shadow puppet play. The burly door guard rose from his seat and hefted short twin batons.

"Look!" Anari hissed. "There's no need for this! You can have it all, just give me a place to stay for a few days."

"Fool," Musa muttered, so quietly that nobody but Anari would know he'd even spoken.

That was when the first blow of the baton landed, as the door guard delivered a strike to the back of Anari's knees. Anari staggered. The door guard's baton swung around to smash into Anari's chest, knocking him down. The door guard set aside his batons and drew a knife. Anari pulled in a breath to declare his true identity and take his chances.

"Of course, we would not soil our hands by killing a Scorned one," the door guard rumbled above him. "Not unless it was accidental because he wouldn't *hold still.*"

Anari held still. He tensed when he felt the knife blade slide into his pocket. It was almost a relief to hear the rasp of the blade cutting through his robe. A moment later, his purse clanked to the hostel floor.

"There's no way that's honest money!" he heard one of the guests say. "We should teach that Scorned one a lesson about stealing from his betters."

The weight lifted from Anari's back. He rose quickly, pivoting to face the threat.

Musa jerked his head toward the door.

Anari made no attempt to retrieve his purse as he left.

Rasee did not look surprised at his abrupt reappearance. She shook her head when he stumbled across the street to her.

"Should have taken that coin you offered," she said ruefully. "Then we'd have money to get something to eat. It does us no good now."

The guard who had escorted Anari out stood in the doorway of the hostel, his arms crossed over his chest. He cleared his throat. When Rasee looked at him, he jerked his head to the side, though he never met her eyes.

"Or maybe it does," she said. She strode to the alley entrance beside the hostel.

"What?" Anari trailed behind her.

"You were lucky," she told him. "There's folks who would have killed you for setting foot inside their places. Fat Musa is a decent man. He doesn't persecute us, and he tries to give value for value within the strictures of what is allowed. Aha!"

She pounced upon a pile beside the back door of the hostel with cries of delight. "Three heavy blankets, a bundle of firewood, and a whole basket filled with food! Even meat! How much money did you lose?"

"More than would buy all this," he said, irritated by her pleasure in what he thought to be a very poor trade.

She raised one eyebrow. "The Scorned aren't allowed to buy anything, so how would you know what it would cost?" Without waiting for an answer, she continued, "Besides, since the war got worse, the cost of food goes up near every day. The Marked aren't as likely to be generous to beggars. Our family will be happy to see this feast."

She scooped up the offering and practically danced away. Anari followed because Rasee was the only person in this city who had proved herself friendly. The Fourth Virtue of the Crow: Remembering Friend and Foe. *The crow studies people until he knows friend from foe. Once known, he will never forget.*

Rasee finally stopped walking at an old brick bridge guarding a dry streambed. Anari leaned against the parapet wall. He straightened when she called out, "I'm home!"

"Rasee?" a woman's voice echoed under the bridge.

A young man poked his head out from behind one of the pilings. "Rasee's back," he called as soon as he saw her.

People tumbled out of the shadows under the brick bridge. They flocked to Rasee like they truly were the family she'd named them.

Rasee's "family" was made up of about a dozen people. Their hands and faces were clean, but they wore ill-fitting, much-mended clothes that were so old that Anari found it difficult to tell what colors they had originally been. They ranged in age from a little white-haired girl who was just beginning to toddle around, to an elderly person so heavily swathed in layers of robes and scarves, despite the heat, that Anari could not guess if they were man, woman, or hijra.

Rasee grinned at a boy who had the barrel-chested, long-limbed build of House Locust but House Fox's signature orange hair. Despite their lack of Band tattoos, most Scorned ones seemed to be cursed by an overabundance of House traits. A woman with the strong jaw of House Horse set down the lantern she carried and hugged Rasee. Anari saw that her hands bore the thickened nails of House Hyena. A few had the same jet black hair or eyes as Anari. Their mixed nature left him unable to guess what they would do next. It made him feel ill.

Not all the Scorned bore the signs of mixed Houses, though. There were just as many who showed the traits of only one House. Anari distrusted them the most, because the reason for their Scorning was not written on their faces for all to see.

An excited murmur rose when the Scorned saw the basket of food and the blankets.

"He's responsible for this," Rasee told them, pointing to Anari.

She proceeded to tell the story of how he had thought that he could rent a room from Fat Musa. She told it as a slapstick comedy, as if Anari hadn't lost his means for surviving and been in fear for his life. She could have been telling the humorous fable of the foolish Scorned one who got three wishes and squandered them all, using the last to restore things to the way they were in the beginning. The Scorned one ended with nothing, still dependent on the charity of others. The fable did not seem so funny anymore.

Rasee's audience laughed at the end of her story, but not unkindly.

"Your loss is a gain for all of us," said a youth who had listened to Rasee with the perfectly motionless focus of House Viper. "That's better than we usually get. Welcome. I am Jian."

Anari extended his hand in greeting, only to realize that he was alone in doing so. It jarred him, like putting his foot through a step that wasn't there. Of course the Scorned did not have tattoos to acknowledge in greeting, and if they touched the wrong person, they would suffer. The habit of clasping hands was a dangerous one for them. Anari converted his movement to scratching a non-existent itch on the side of his nose.

Touching his face woke the pain from his eye. It radiated across his hot, swollen cheek. Rasee's compress had dried out, and the benefit it offered had vanished. He left it on anyway, to avoid showing the damage.

The woman with the jaw of a Horse and the fingernails of a Hyena interrupted before Anari could introduce himself in turn.

"We will all have time to introduce ourselves. But when there is food, we eat!"

"Yes, Galilahi," Jian said.

From the tone in Jian's voice, and the murmur of laughter that ran through the group, Anari guessed that, "Yes, Galilahi," was an oft-repeated refrain.

Anari was too shocked to laugh with them. Despite her mixed traits and House Horse name, Galilahi's statement could have come straight from the Advantages of the Hyena. *Advantage One: The hyena does not waste. If he has food, he will eat it at once.* Anari had seen that Scorned ones could share some of the Dangers of their progenitors' Houses, yes, but he hadn't expected the same to be true of the Advantages.

"Can we have a fire?" Rasee asked. "There's no fire allowed on the ship. I missed it. It might be the dry season on land, but nothing ever stayed truly dry shipboard."

Galilahi smiled. "Yes," she told them all. "We will not sleep cold tonight. We have enough wood for a fire, and we can celebrate Rasee's return with a feast!"

She shooed the motley family about its duties with a wave of her hand. Rasee and the children went to get the eating platters, cups, and drinking water. A couple of the adults rounded up the littlest ones.

"Your basket is very welcome," Galilahi told Anari, once she'd set the others to their tasks. She picked up the blankets and handed them to Anari. "Carry these for me. One is for you. The nights get chilly. The other two will go to Calogero. He's badly injured, and cold nights are hardest for him." She hefted the firewood and the basket of food. She walked away without checking to make sure that Anari followed.

He did. She seemed to actually know what she was doing, unlike him.

"Calogero, good news!" she said, approaching a man huddled on the ground beside one of the bridge supports. "I have blankets for you, and tonight we will have fire and food."

"Trying to keep me alive a little bit longer, are you?"

The faint accent of the voice was strangely familiar, but Anari couldn't place it. It felt like he'd heard it long ago, or in a fever dream. The man pushed himself up with one hand, cradling the other against his stomach. He wore light blue robes spoiled with stains and crude patches. Rags wrapped his injured hand.

Recognition stunned Anari. This was the Scorned one that he'd seen across the river during the burning of his seed-father's body. The one who had dared to speak to him after the oba's funeral. He'd grabbed the reins of the horse. If he'd polluted the House Crow healer, Anari would have died. A flush of rage filled Anari. He wanted to scream at the man, to demand he beg forgiveness for his crime. He fought down the urge, but the effort held him immobile.

Galilahi took two of the blankets from his arms as

if nothing were wrong. She tucked one across Calogero's lap and draped the other over his shoulders.

"Well, you make such a good beggar now," Galilahi said briskly, answering Calogero. "It would be a shame to lose that ability before its time."

Calogero chuckled hoarsely. His expression didn't change when he met Anari's gaze. Of course, he'd last seen Anari wearing his finest palace clothing and still in possession of both eyes. Anari had looked different then, better, even poisoned and half-unconscious.

Anari reminded himself of the Fourth Virtue of the Crow. He did not yet know if Calogero was a friend or a foe, so he would treat him as neutral until he acted otherwise.

"We have him to thank for the blankets and firewood, and food too," Galilahi told Calogero. She knelt and began laying the fire.

"All this? He must have sacrificed much to receive such bounty."

Galilahi nodded. "It's getting harder and harder," she told Anari. "There are not so many people willing to give or trade food to us anymore. I heard two warriors talking; they said that the infidels have begun burning fields and salting the ground, so that even when our warriors drive them back, the crops and the land are ruined." She shook her head as she kindled the fire. "I don't understand why the infidels are doing it. It hurts them as much as us."

"They're desperate," Calogero said. "They think if they hurt the Eight Houses enough, the oba will agree to talk with them. They do not understand that they are Scorned. They do not understand that if anybody, even the oba himself, speaks with them, that person will be cast out of his House. They cannot return home. And so they die." Calogero's voice faded as he finished.

A tongue of firelight licked up the underside of the brick bridge, illuminating the chinks in its mortar. The crackle of burning green wood sounded strange when distorted by the bridge's echo, but the familiar smell of the fire evoked Anari's hearth at home. It comforted him, until he remembered that that home was no longer his.

Anari was leaning against a piling, his feet warm from the fire and his belly full of meat and bread, when Galilahi spoke again.

"Now that we've eaten," she said, "let us all introduce ourselves. As hosts, we should go first. I am Galilahi. My mother was a Scorned one, and I do not know my seed-father. Leotie," she pointed to the white-haired toddler, "is my daughter. It was dark when he took me, but I think her seed-father was of House Horse. She has the gray coloring."

Anari felt heat in his cheeks. It was not from embarrassment, but from shame. He was ashamed that a member of one of the Eight Houses would behave so despicably toward a defenseless Scorned one. And he was ashamed that his first thought had been, "How could he lower himself like that? To consort with a Scorned one?" He pushed his guilt aside by concentrating on what she was saying.

"I do fine piecework and mending," she finished. She looked to her right, to Calogero. He had curled up in his blankets, his eyes glazed as he stared into the fire. She nudged him. After he blinked the glaze from his eyes, she gently said, "Introduction time."

"I am Calogero," he said, "and mine is a simple story. I was a ninth child. My parents did not take me to a priest to have my hand tattooed when I was two weeks old, and so I am a Scorned one. I was born outside Alhadd. I went to Ayeli Asatsvyi hoping to be able to make a living doing work that I was suited for, but I failed. I failed miserably." He lifted his crippled hand in illustration.

Had he recognized Anari after all?

"I had failed, and I was no longer safe in Ayeli Asatsvyi. I left and came here a few days ago. Jian found me and brought me here. Now I beg in the streets." He shrugged. "In truth, it is not so different from the work I had planned."

Anari waited for Calogero to denounce him, but Calogero only turned to the man on his right. The man said, "My name is Poul."

Anari listened to Poul's introduction and to the introductions of those who followed. He tried to remember their names. It made it easier if he could think of them by name. Each gave the reason that they were Scorned, and each ended by explaining how they survived.

Every person had a different way of surviving: Galilahi did fine needlework for dress shops; Rasee worked as crew aboard the ship that he'd met her on— "The captain is a cousin of my father," she explained; Calogero begged; Poul pulled a dung cart; and Jian made delicate carvings that would be sold without his name attached to them.

When Jian displayed one of the pieces he was working on, a frog catching a fly, Anari stared, dumbfounded. He recognized the style of the detail work that scrolled around the fly's wings. His mother owned a carving of a fledgling crow that had been made by the same artisan. The merchant that she had bought it from had insisted that it was done by an isolated master carver living in the mountains. It was how he justified the high price.

After the last of the Scorned had finished his story, all faces turned expectantly to Anari.

"My name is An—," he stopped himself just before he said his real name, "—Anaadi. My birth wasn't sanctioned. My mother died giving birth because she refused to allow the priests to be called, but my guide-father was rich and powerful. He hired tutors for me and raised me secretly. Then he died, and his family threw me out to survive on my own."

Rasee had given Anari the seed of his disguise. "You haven't been on your own long, have you?" she'd asked. "Your family kept you. They hid you as long as they could."

Anari knew he couldn't pass as one who had been treated as Scorned from birth. He would make too many mistakes. He'd never heard of anyone keeping a child born without the sanction of the gods, but the glowing faces surrounding him confirmed that this was a tale the Scorned wanted to believe. Calogero grimaced, but that might have been from the pain. Only Galilahi's expression remained unchanged.

"I accidentally ended up on the battlefield." Anari paused, to let their imaginations fill in the rest. "Rasee found me nearby," he continued. "I was feverish from my wound." He waved his hand toward the compress over his eye. "She saved my life."

He waited as the silence grew. Did they not believe him?

"And how will you provide for yourself?" Galilahi prompted him. "We cannot support you. Rasee told me that the money you had was taken from you, which is how we received this feast. Tomorrow, you must earn your own dinner. It is not as if we can eat a temple's charity meal when we can't fill our bellies."

Anari couldn't exactly tell them that he only needed to worry about it for another three days. Besides, he'd be very hungry by then.

He could calculate the supplies a standing army would consume, he could devise battle strategies, he could quote every line from the Books of Law, he knew the Ways of the Crow by heart, he knew what the Advantages and Dangers of each House were and how to detect their signs, he knew how to make rulings that would be seen as fair and merciful ... and none of it would help him to survive now.

"Well?" Galilahi asked. "If need be, Poul can teach you the dung trade, but you will have to find a way to get your own cart."

Even if nobody ever found out about it, even if he were going into exile, the Crow royal heir *could not* push a dung cart. It would be the final blow to Anari's shattered dignity. He scrambled to think of something less humiliating that a Scorned one might do.

"I can sing," he said finally, after there had been no sound but the crackling of the fire for several minutes.

He was not an amazing singer. That was not a Virtue of House Crow, though some of the songbird Bands under Lord Crow's wing did have beautiful voices. He had been taught how to sing, though, as part of the proper upbringing for a man.

"That's good," Galilahi said, smiling. "Beggars do best when they can show off a skill *and* a horrifying affliction."

She leaned across and lifted his eye compress. She didn't flinch when she saw the ruin of his eye. "Yes, that will do nicely."

She was right, and he hated it.

"Calogero will take you with him tomorrow morning, to teach you the way of it." She stood and clapped her hands. "To sleep! For once, we may dream about something other than food."

Wrapped in a blanket beside the embers of the dying fire, Anari slept soundly until a shadowy sweep of wing pulled him into dreaming. He heard the rustle of feathers, and then Lord Crow stood beside him.

"Have you decided what your wish will be?" Lord Crow asked.

He sounded almost bored, and Anari's skin prickled with alarm. A bored god was a dangerous thing. Anari shook his head, unwilling to risk speech.

Lord Crow craned his neck to consider himself. "It must be soon," he told Anari. "My feather will not grow back until you use your favor. The bald spot is very unflattering, and I have a certain beauty that I'm trying to impress. Come now! Do you want your eye back? Your rival punished? Treasure? A sign of my favor?"

Anari held perfectly still, afraid to even blink, lest Lord Crow take it as agreement. He was not about to agree to anything in a dream, not when there were so many ways for it to turn into a trick.

Lord Crow tilted his head and eyed Anari. He drummed his fingers against the ground. "Not now? You must choose soon. Very soon."

The drumming of Lord Crow's fingers sounded like a beak pecking a snail shell. At Anari's thought, a snail appeared beneath the god's hand. Lord Crow laughed in surprise, tossed the snail into the air, and caught it in his mouth with a ferocious snap of teeth that shattered the snail's shell.

After he swallowed the snail, broken bits of shell

and all, Lord Crow said, "I have decided. You must choose your favor before your role in the succession is settled. If you do not, I will choose it for you."

Before Anari could protest, Lord Crow unfurled his shadow wings and flew away.

Anari woke with a start. By the dimming light of the fire, he saw that all the Scorned were curled up with their eyes closed. In three days, the final challenge between the royal heirs would take place in Ayeli Asatsvyi. In three days, Anari had to ask a favor of a trickster god.

Sleep did not come to him as easily the second time.

When Calogero woke him the next morning, Anari was cold and thirsty. His eye burned, and his stomach growled. Faint streaks of pink scratched the sky.

"Let's be going, Anaadi," Calogero said. In the morning, his eyes were clear and sharp. He moved with purpose, though he still cradled his mutilated hand against his belly.

Anari stared blankly at him until he remembered that he'd given his name as Anaadi the night before.

"Drink up." Calogero offered him a tin cup of water.

Anari did not inquire about breakfast, but Calogero mentioned it anyway.

"The others say that they used to have leftover bread for breakfast. Now, too often we don't even have a crust for dinner."

Anari drained the cup and rose to his feet. The world spun around him. His legs wobbled. He stood still until the feeling of weakness passed, at which point another imperative made itself known.

"Where do you——?" he gestured at his nether

regions.

Calogero pointed along the dry streambed. "Around the curve. Shout first, to make sure you don't disturb someone else. Remember to aim downhill, and if you're making a pile, use the shovel to lift it into the dung cart after."

The shocking touch of cold morning air on his sensitive bits woke Anari all the way up. It felt good to relieve his bladder, until he looked down. Blood dyed his puddle of piss pink. Two days. All he had to do was survive two more days, and then whatever lingering damage he'd suffered from the poison could be healed. The pain from his eye would end, though his eye could not be restored.

He used the shovel from the dung cart to cover up the tell-tale pink stain on the ground.

He hurried away from the evidence, but the ground beneath his feet felt fragile, as if it might give way at any moment.

"You're quick. Good," Calogero greeted him. "We have some distance to go, and it's best to be out of the way when respectable Marked need to use the streets."

They made it to the bazaar just as the traders were setting up their stalls for the day, unrolling their straw mats, building pyramids of cassava tubers and green okra pods and other foods, and setting out bowls heaped high with an aromatic sunrise of red and gold spices.

Calogero made a satisfied sound and dragged Anari to squat in the dirt beneath a tall, spindly neem tree with an outrageous shock of bright green leaves sprouting directly above them.

"Perfect," he said to Anari. "We have our spot, and we're settled. You see, we are in a place that nobody else could possibly want. There's nothing to sit on, and there won't even be any shade for most of the day. But!" He raised one finger and winked at Anari. "The tree will give us shade in the hottest part of the day, and many will walk that path in front of us, so it is an excellent place for beggars."

Anari found the level of foresight and planning on Calogero's part unnerving. He told himself to be fair. He would have found such strategizing normal in the palace; he was merely shocked because Calogero was a Scorned one.

Anari sang. Calogero spoke. They took turns. When the strain of performing while injured exhausted them both at the same time, they fell silent until one recovered enough strength to continue. Calogero had a silver tongue equal to any that Anari had ever heard. He quoted the First Virtue of the Horse: Calmness when a horse trader walked by. The trader realized that Anari's singing had soothed a skittish bay mare, and Anari found himself the recipient of a handful of brass bits. A paean of praise to wisdom and kindness of those who follow the Third Virtue of the Rat: Charity won them two thumb-sized blocks of scented sandalwood from a carpenter. Calogero quickly tucked those away under his robes.

A servant was jostled by a man with the narrow-set eyes and strong jaw line of Band Mule, House Horse. The man didn't even look to see who he'd shoved aside, much less apologize. Calogero made a scathing comment about a mule so intent on the carrot dangled in front of him that he ignored the bountiful field he trampled over. The servant laughed, her good humor and vanity restored, and set a paper-wrapped package in their begging bowl.

Unwrapped, the package proved to hold three flatbreads stuffed with curried potatoes and greens. "Lunch," Calogero said. He didn't sound as excited about it as Anari would have expected.

Calogero hefted their empty water flask. "There's a well on the far side of the bazaar that I may be allowed to use," he told Anari. "The water tastes bad, but it won't make us sick. Keep singing; you have the way of it."

Anari nodded and launched into a hymn in praise of the gods. The Locust priest who was inspecting a bolt of silk nodded approvingly, but he didn't glance in Anari's direction. To Anari's surprise, he found that he was enjoying himself. He'd rarely had the opportunity to observe the common people. He found it fascinating, even though he had to do it covertly from the lowly position of one of the Scorned. Besides, the sky was blue, the air was fresh, and he liked to sing.

He was singing with his eyes downcast to avoid eye contact that might be taken as an insult, when three pairs of sandals stopped in front of him. "What a fine day to hear an epic song," a young man commented languidly, as if to his companions.

"Indeed," another agreed. "Something to stir the blood for war!"

Anari glanced up. Three young men of House Locust stood a few feet away. None of them looked directly at him, but they were clearly waiting.

Anari scoured his memory. Battle songs were not part of the repertoire of House Crow, but he knew a couple. He settled on "From Victory to the Wheel," wherein a victorious dying warrior lists all the things that his death has protected—his House, his Band, his home, his child—and proclaims that it was worth it. His spirit is fulfilled and he is ready to move forward on the wheel. Old warriors could never listen to it without getting a tear in their eye.

Anari had only made it as far as the refrain when a kick to his ribs knocked the wind out of him and sent the flatbread in his lap flying.

"We do not want a song about *dying*," growled one of the young men.

They closed in around him. Anari's mind raced. He could fight them off—maybe. His damaged eye made distances impossible to judge. If he did fight, he would certainly draw attention. The Scorned were not allowed to learn to fight, much less win.

"Such brave warriors should not waste their efforts on a worthless Scorned one!" Anari cried.

They hesitated.

"Warriors need their strength for the battlefield." The moment Anari said it, he knew that he'd gone one step too far.

Their mouths twisted. A mean glint entered their eyes. Their hands knotted into fists.

"Oh, no," said a loud voice, pitched to project. "What a tragedy, to see godly men pollute themselves by touching a Scorned one! How unpleasant and risky the purification ritual that they must endure. How costly it is, to their souls and their purses. Fifteen rupiyas are not easily spared in these difficult times. If they cannot tithe that sum to a priest for the purification of their souls, then they may themselves become Scorned. A tragedy!"

The young men surrounding Anari hesitated. The Locust priest who had been bargaining for a bolt of silk raised his head in sudden interest at the mention of tithing. The men must have seen the priest as well, because they left in a hurry.

Calogero knelt beside Anari. "Are you injured?" he asked.

Anari shook his head. His ribs throbbed, waking sympathetic pain in his joints. Everything hurt more than it should because of the lingering effects of the poison, but he could endure it for another couple of days until it could be banished. It was nothing compared to the soul-sickness that he felt. "Not a single person raised their hand to stop those three. Is there not a drop of charity or kindness in the Eight Houses? Do we deserve to be destroyed?" He raised his face to Calogero. "Why were they like that?"

"They're scared," Calogero told him. "Those three—I'm guessing that they were recently told they must go out and defend their country. They asked for a battle song, didn't they?"

Anari nodded.

"Those who watched and did nothing …" Calogero lowered his brows. "When times are difficult, people become less willing to put themselves out for others. When your son died two months ago and you are the only one protecting your granddaughter, you are less likely to risk getting hurt by stepping into someone else's fight. When you're worried about the rising cost of food, you're less likely to give bread to a beggar."

"This is all because of the war?"

Calogero shook his head. "Not all, no. It just makes everything worse. Now come, get up! We are done here for the day. The priest has bought his cloth and left. If those young men change their minds and come back, they will find nothing to stop them." He picked up the flatbread from the dirt, dusted it off, and tucked it away in his robe.

At first, Anari's concentration was taken up by the effort of keeping his breathing shallow and painless as he walked. Gradually, he was able to take deeper and deeper breaths, until he was breathing normally.

"Calogero," he said suddenly, "how did you know that House Locust's fine for touching a Scorned one would be fifteen rupiyas?"

Calogero shrugged, continuing to look ahead. "Coincidence?" he suggested.

"No," Anari said. "Every House sets its penalties differently. Few people would know what another House's penalties are. A Scorned one has no reason at all to have that information."

"I just proved differently," Calogero said lightly.

"What are you?" Anari demanded, stopping in the street. "You're no ordinary Scorned one."

"Neither are you, Eye," Calogero said in an undertone, "but I suggest that we wait to have this conversation until we are sure that we will not be overheard."

Suddenly, every shadow became a hiding place for spies. Anari kept his mouth shut until they were near the old brick bridge.

"You did recognize me," he said.

"I could hardly forget the cost of our first introduction." Calogero wore an odd smile, like he was laughing at a bitter private joke. He caressed his maimed hand.

"Why didn't you turn me in to House Raven? I'm sure there's a reward."

"Based on your experience as a Scorned one," Calogero asked, "do you think they would give it to me? Besides, I suspect that there might be advantages to not turning you in." He kept that weird half-smile. "It's a slight chance, but more than I had before."

"I don't understand."

"That would be my cue to answer your first question. You were trained to wear the beaded crown. Do you know what an ambassador is?"

Anari reflexively hooked his thumbs and spread his fingers to invoke the protection of Lord Crow. "They are a trick by the infidels. They are sent to lure our rulers and advisors into speaking with them. They try to weaken us by making our leaders Scorned."

"That isn't how we see it."

"What?" Anari gasped.

"What I told you was not a lie," Calogero said. "I was a ninth child. I was born far outside Alhadd, on the other side of the border and across the desert land bridge. My parents did not take me to a priest to be tattooed, but it was not because they abandoned me. It was because we do not follow your House gods. We have our own gods. Here that makes me Scorned."

Calogero's odd, unHousely appearance made sense now. Anari shook his head, not in denial, but in shock.

"I served for years as an ambassador, figuring out what exchanges your ambassadors—your border priests—would make. Communicating with them, in a way, even if they never spoke a word. When things got bad, I came here hoping to keep our two countries from war. I failed. Your oba would not speak to me. Nobody would speak to me. I learned what it meant to be Scorned. I learned that your oba would never speak with any of my people. I told our rulers this. All our ambassadors did. They could not accept it. They were desperate, and so they attacked. They still believe that if they hurt you enough, you will have to speak to them." He shrugged, and his mouth twisted. "I had failed, but

I came back. My wife died of the Great Plague while I was gone. I had nothing to stay home for, and I suppose I had not given up all hope after all. And then I learned that after the oba died, the royal heirs would be exempt from your people's insane prohibition against speaking to anyone you consider 'Scorned'. You seemed less dangerous to contact than some of the other heirs, or so I thought."

Anari frowned. As was the custom of the royal heirs, he had frequently watched from behind a carved wooden screen as his seed-father met with his advisors. "Your country is ravaged by a plague," he said, remembering.

"Yes. Nobody has been left untouched, but the Great Plague continues." Calogero closed his eyes for a moment. "We know that the rats cause the plague, but all our efforts cannot rid us of them. You have rats too. By all logic, you should also be suffering from the Great Plague, but you are not." He glared at Anari. "You live while our families die! If you told us how to avoid the plague, we would go away and leave you in peace. And yet you will not speak to us, will not even listen to us." He stopped, breathing heavily. After his voice was under control again, he finished. "So we fight, and both sides die."

"It isn't that simple," Anari said. There was a lump in his throat that made it difficult to speak. "As one of the royal heirs, I learned the responsibilities of all the gods. I can tell you why the plague doesn't touch us, but it won't do you any good."

Calogero seized Anari's shoulders. "Tell me," he demanded.

"Lord Rat," Anari said. "He extends his protection over all the Houses. Everywhere the people of the

Eight Houses live, Lord Rat cleanses the rats of pests that cause illness."

It was another blessing that Anari would give up when he went into exile. He'd thought of it only in terms of having to leave the royal household and endure the infidel Scorned, but the protections of his House would be stripped from him. He wouldn't even be able to protect those members of his House who went into exile with him. They would all share the risks of the Scorned. They might die of a pest-borne plague. *He* might die of it.

"Your gods." Calogero stared at him and then laughed. "Your gods save you from the Great Plague. Your gods, whose stupid rules are the reason that you die on the battlefield."

"Would you have believed us?" Anari asked. "Even if we had told you?"

"We couldn't. I can't. You are our last chance. The war will go on until we are all dead, of plague or battle, but my people will not go alone."

Anari met Calogero's eyes. He had nothing to offer. The day after tomorrow, one of the other royal heirs would be crowned oba. Anari would go into exile over the mountains, away from the Eight Houses and their war with Calogero's people. Those who stayed behind would be the ones suffering, not him.

"Here." Calogero handed Anari the battered packet of flatbread.

Anari unwrapped the paper and tore the flatbread in half. He offered half to Calogero.

"You keep it. I don't have much appetite after noon." Calogero shuffled to his spot under the bridge, wrapped himself in his blankets despite the heat of midday, and faced the wall.

Anari sat in the shade and waited for the others to return. The flatbread and the curried potatoes it was stuffed with were delicious, which only made him feel worse.

Grim thoughts trailed him through the day like an invisible funeral procession. They made poor company, but they wouldn't leave him alone. Long after the others had fallen asleep, Anari stayed awake, staring at the stars above him. He watched them move through their intricate dance across the inky night sky.

When he woke, the sky was lightening to blue. He felt as though he had just fallen asleep. A thin sliver of sun clipped the horizon. A new day had begun: the day before the challenge for oba.

"What do you want most?" a voice demanded.

Anari rose and turned. "Lord Crow," he said respectfully. "I do not wish to use my favor yet. I still have time to decide."

Lord Crow shivered his skin irritably. The hiss of shifting feathers filled the air. He tilted his head and stared at Anari with eyes whose black stretched from corner to corner. "I warned you. You must choose your favor before your role in the succession is settled. If you don't, I will choose for you. You are lucky I'm giving you that much time. The other gods mock me for missing a feather."

"I will choose before the end of the succession challenge," Anari promised.

Lord Crow craned his neck. "This is not Ayeli Asatsvyi. What are you still doing here?"

Anari blinked. The cold morning breeze whispered past his ear like a warning. "I am waiting for the succession challenge to end, so that I can safely accept exile," he said slowly.

"Boring. Are you sure?"

Of course. You have never shown me any mark of special favor. I don't have a chance of winning. "Why?"

"If you are certain that you will accept exile, then your role in the succession is settled." Lord Crow pinned Anari under a beady gaze.

Shock reverberated through Anari like the *crack* of a shattering snail shell.

"Name your favor now, or I'll choose it for you."

"No!"

Lord Crow tilted his head. "No?"

Anari scrabbled to pull his thoughts together. "No, I am not certain I will accept exile."

Lord Crow grinned, flashing ferociously sharp teeth. "Then I expect to see you at the challenge. And don't forget, you have a mark of my favor now."

Anari pressed his hand to the royal Crow birthmark on his chest. One wing fluttered like a butterfly against his palm as the favor struggled to escape.

Lord Crow waved his arm in a broad gesture, trailed by a wing of shadow. "If you do not wish to go alone, you may bring these ones with you as your flock."

Anari looked behind him. The sound of voices had roused the Scorned. They stared, eyes wide and mouths gaping. Though it was well within his power, Lord Crow had not seen fit to keep their conversation private.

"Why—?" Anari began to ask Lord Crow. He found himself talking to thin air.

Silence poured in, the kind of silence that promises shouting.

Anari faced the Scorned. "I lied earlier."

"Yes," Galilahi answered. She didn't appear surprised.

"I helped you. I saved your life, and you lied to us," Rasee accused him.

"I'm sorry. My name is Anari. I am the royal heir of House Crow. I wanted to hide until the succession challenge ended and I could go into exile, but things went wrong. I ended up wounded on the battlefield. Rasee, you *did* save my life. You have all saved my life by letting me stay among you. I'm in danger. Others have tried to kill me."

"So you hide," Galilahi said. There was no judgment in her tone, but Anari felt compelled to explain.

"I don't have any power to protect myself," he said. "I'm not favored by Lord Crow. I can't be oba."

Disbelief rested in every furrowed brow and frowning face.

"I don't have any power," Anari repeated. Then he remembered who he was speaking to. He winced. Compared to the Scorned, he had incredible power. Power like the ability to rent a room.

"We knew you lied," Galilahi said. "Scorned children are not hidden away and cherished and tutored until they are grown."

Rasee made a small protesting noise. Galilahi ignored it.

"It's a beautiful dream," she said, "but there's no substance to it. It can't fill our bellies or keep us warm on cold nights."

That, Anari could do something about.

"I have to get to Ayeli Asatsvyi for the succession challenge tomorrow. If you come with me, I'll see to it that you are generously rewarded."

"If you win the challenge, you won't even be able to speak with us," Calogero pointed out. He didn't sound as if he cared one way or the other. Sweat beaded on his skin despite the cool morning air, and rosy streaks blossomed along his wounded arm. He stared at Anari with fever-bright eyes.

"I don't expect to win," Anari said. "But you will be rewarded either way, I promise."

"Usually the promise of a rich reward for a Scorned one is only another dream," Galilahi said, "but I believe you this time."

"Thank you," Anari said.

"How do you plan on getting us there?"

"I—" Anari stopped. "Rasee, will your father's cousin take us all as passengers on his ship? I will pay for our passage and any tithes for purification."

Her face crumpled. "He would, but he isn't here. He's collecting a shipment of dried corn and taking it to the south to trade."

"Where?"

"The place where he's loading the ship is a day's travel by foot. He won't be back for at least a week."

"That's too late."

"I know of a camel racer who might be persuaded to take a message to the captain, for the right payment," Calogero offered, his tone distant.

Payment. The word tickled Anari's memory. "Jian, who do you sell your carvings to?"

"Egil of House Fox, Band Dhole. Why?" Jian asked.

"Because he's charging a very high price for them and lying about where they came from. To keep that knowledge private, he'll be willing to pay enough to hire a messenger. How do you meet him when you have something new to sell?"

"He sees me at the back door of his shop. Today is Foxday. His shop is closed. He will be at home with his family. Their door guard won't let a Scorned one through the gate."

Anari's mind raced. As he thought, his eyes followed the curve of the dry streambed. Around the bend was the place where the Scorned emptied their bladders and bowels, he remembered. Then he had it. "Everyone shits, whether it's their holy day or not. We have Poul's dung cart. That's our way in."

7

THE NEXT DAY, after a long boat ride, they waited in front of the palace gates in Ayeli Asatsvyi. Rasee fidgeted from foot to foot like a child who had to pee. "They won't let us in."

"Yes, they will." Anari summoned his old instinctive arrogance and used it to put conviction into his voice.

"We're late."

"The challenge doesn't end until the sun is directly overhead. We are *not* late. We made it from Alhadd to Ayeli Asatsvyi. We made it to the palace. They will let us in." Anari gripped the palace gate's metal bars and shook vigorously, making a racket that should bring the gate guards running.

"It will be fine even if they only let you in," Galilahi said. "I trust you. We can wait for our reward outside. It's nothing new."

"Lord Crow said that I could bring you with me. He will make sure that you are allowed inside. This should be simple." Anari hoped that was true. He wanted them to see that Crow promises would be kept, even when they were made to Scorned ones.

"As simple as it was to get the money from Egil?" Jian asked. "He's never going to forget that, not after what happened. We'll have to move to a different city."

"That was not how most families spend their holy day," Anari said.

Rasee shuddered. "The peacock!"

"Nobody could have predicted that peacock," Galilahi said firmly.

A man sprinted from the palace to the locked gate. Even if he hadn't emerged from the Viper royal wing of the palace, the speed of his movement would have given away his House.

"Eye of House Crow," he greeted Anari. "You and your … others … are welcome."

He unlocked the gate and held it open for them.

Anari strode through as if he had never doubted that they would be allowed in. He ignored the way the effort made his right leg shake. A few poison-induced muscle tremors couldn't stop him now.

Once they were past the gate guard, Anari told the others, "The succession challenge is held in the Mango Courtyard. Try to stay silent no matter what you see."

"What will you be doing?" asked Calogero. The infidel's voice came out as a harsh croak, and he swayed as he walked. Only Rasee's support kept him walking in more or less the same direction as the rest of them.

Anari didn't answer.

As they passed under the shadows of the mango trees, a breeze ruffled the glossy dark green leaves.

"You are here, and with your little flock." Lord Crow studied Anari with one beady eye and then the other. "I had planned what favor I would give you if you didn't show up, too."

Anari shuddered.

"You are one of mine. And you are at a disadvantage, because of what another one of mine took. I can't have that."

Lord Crow ripped away the cloth that Anari wore over his ruined right eye. He placed a hand on the ravaged eye socket. Pain lanced through Anari's skull. He screamed. Tears washed down his cheeks.

The agony vanished as suddenly as it had appeared. Anari blinked—and realized that he could see with both eyes again.

"I did not ask to be healed!"

"Don't worry. This isn't a favor." Lord Crow cocked his head and stared up at the trees above them. "Do you think the mangoes are ripe yet?"

"The mangoes," Anari repeated, bewildered by the question.

Lord Crow leapt into the air. His shadow wings unfurled with a snap that set plumes of dust dancing.

Anari threw up his arm to shield his eye—his *eyes*, he thought in wonder. When he lowered his arm, Lord Crow was gone and everyone was staring at him.

"I can see," he told them.

They nodded, still staring. Finally, Rasee spoke.

"You— Your eye—" Words failed her. She took a small disc of polished metal from her skirt pocket and extended it to him.

Anari nearly dropped the mirror when he saw his own reflection. His right eye had been, not restored, but replaced. It was black from one edge to the other, like the eyes of Lord Crow.

"Nobody can argue that you don't have a sign of favor from Lord Crow now," Calogero said.

Anari glanced in his direction and flinched. Two

Calogeros looked back at him, layered over each other like a reflection in a lake and the reality underneath. One was Calogero as he had appeared moments earlier. The other regarded Anari from sunken dead eyes, its lips pulled back in a skeleton grin. Pus-filled abscesses pocked the ghost's swollen organs. When Anari focused on it, the image of the ghostly corpse sharpened.

Pain jabbed between Anari's eyes. He glanced wildly from person to person, but only Calogero appeared transformed. Nobody else had even noticed. Rasee still held Calogero's arm across her shoulders. She stared at Anari as if he were the one who had something wrong with him.

"Lord Crow's act was not a favor," Anari managed to say. At least the double vision only afflicted him when he looked at Calogero. His head throbbed as he led the way through the grove of mango trees to the succession challenge. He did not look behind him.

As they entered the Mango Courtyard, the first thing Anari saw was a woman sprawled in its center. Xixu of House Viper held the same stillness she always had in repose, but this time it was the stillness of death. Gouges pockmarked her face. Her eyes were bloody ruins. A huge black raven perched on her head.

Witnesses from the Eight Houses ringed the courtyard. The members of House Viper were as motionless as their dead royal heir. Their faces could have been carved from stone.

A priest of House Fox stood in front of the witnesses from his House. He held the beaded crown.

Kayin sat on the ground a few feet away. Blood spattered his face. His gaze was hard as he looked for other challengers.

There were none.

Ahyoka knelt in submission at the edge of the courtyard in front of House Horse, her gaze directed at the ground. Blood matted her hair and she cradled her left arm. Among the witnesses, the palomino girl she'd chosen to be her second wife kept giving Ahyoka's arm worried looks.

When Anari and the Scorned emerged from the mango trees, a rustle went through the Eight Houses. Anari heard muted gasps.

Some came from House Crow. His mother stared at him, her dark eyes stricken. Romesh stood beside her, but his expression held more interest than shock. As a healer priest of Lord Crow, he must have guessed that something significant had changed when he received word that Scorned ones might accompany Anari to the succession challenge. The head of the household guard looked like he was recalculating odds.

The members of House Raven gazed at Anari. Many of them knew him from when he was a boy trailing behind Kayin, but their sharp black eyes gave nothing away.

Anari searched the House Raven witnesses for Adetosoye. Kayin's guide-father had taught Anari much of what it meant to be a man. Anari still cared about his opinion. Adetosoye was present, but he sat on a stool in the middle of the House Raven crowd. Anari couldn't see him clearly.

At the reaction of the audience, Kayin looked up and saw Anari. "I hoped you were gone," he said.

"I'm not." Anari's throat felt tight from the pressure of words unsaid.

"No, you aren't."

Kayin picked up his sword and rolled to his feet in one smooth movement despite the white bone jutting out of the bottom of his boot.

Anari stared at the bone. His headache flared back to life. He blinked. There was no bone sticking out after all. Kayin's boot was whole and undamaged. The bone's ghostly image floated *over* Kayin's boot. A line of shadow crossed it, like a crack.

Anari studied Kayin.

To Anari's normal eye, the Raven royal heir appeared invincible. He was large and strong and protected by a rich padded velvet coat of armor studded with a thousand brass nails that gleamed in the sunlight. His breastplate and armored thigh plates had been polished to a mirror shine marred only by the dried blood of others. He was armed with sword and ax.

To Anari's other eye, Kayin was carrion-in-waiting. He had a cracked bone in his left foot that would cripple him. Strained muscles and bruised bones lay beneath his armor. His heart beat too fast, laboring to keep him upright.

"Do you concede that I will make the better oba?" Kayin asked.

"No."

Kayin nodded, almost in agreement. "It is the challenge, then."

The head of the Crow household guard stepped forward to present Anari with his own padded coat of armor. As he assisted Anari into it, he murmured, "His left foot is injured. He won't lunge on that foot, so you'll have to guard twice as hard on the other side."

Anari nodded. "I know."

The guard's fingers paused for a moment. He strapped Anari's sword and long dagger into place and stepped back. "Lord Crow be with you."

"He's certainly paying attention." It would have been simpler if he weren't.

As soon as the Fox priest gave the signal to begin, Kayin lunged forward with his sword outstretched to skewer Anari.

Anari stepped in toward Kayin's weak side, letting the sword slide past him. He launched a flurry of blows to distract Kayin and throw him off-balance, but Kayin blocked them with ease despite the stretch-and-tug of injured muscles beneath his armor.

Kayin attacked with broad, strong strokes. Anari ducked and dodged and redirected the blows.

Anari attacked quick and light, targeting the weaknesses that his doubled vision revealed. Kayin blocked every strike, directly absorbing their impact.

A murmur passed through the witnesses when it became apparent that a victor would not be immediately settled. A shift in House Raven's crowd of witnesses allowed Anari to clearly see Adetosoye, Kayin's guide-father.

Adetosoye did not look well even to Anari's ordinary eye. He sat when others stood. He had the bone structure of a big man, but his flesh had wasted away.

To Anari's new eye, he looked worse. His bulk may have dwindled, but new life flourished inside him. Malevolent growths bulged like clusters of ripe figs in his lungs.

Kayin followed the direction of Anari's gaze. His mouth tightened. "Concede," he demanded.

If Anari conceded the challenge, Lord Crow would instantly bestow upon him a "favor" of the god's choosing. If Anari used Lord Crow's favor, he lost any advantage he might have had in reserve.

When Anari didn't answer, Kayin attacked with redoubled strength.

Anari's head throbbed. He didn't dare close his eyes for even a moment to gain some relief. Weakness crept into his limbs as he dodged and blocked. Feeling the lingering effects of his poisoning was bad enough, but his new eye forced him to watch them as well.

He had never beaten Kayin without using Crow tricks, and he only had one trick left. He pressed his free hand to his royal birthmark and the favor that connected him to Lord Crow.

"Lord Crow—" He stopped. His connection to Lord Crow might give him another trick after all, even if it had never worked for him before.

He watched for his chance. The next time Kayin committed to an attack, Anari dove under the strike and rolled forward to get as much distance between them as possible.

Anari knelt on one knee and released a series of screams that mimicked the harsh cry of a crow.

Kayin spun to face him. He lifted his sword.

Anari rose to his feet, keeping his back bowed and his arms curved down like wings. He couldn't tell if it was working. He didn't feel any different. He stomped the rhythm, keeping his elbows up as he swung his arms, letting his upper arms carry the motion.

Kayin charged at him.

Anari raised his sword high and *cawed* as he brought it swinging down diagonally through the air in front of him.

Kayin tumbled backward as if he'd been buffeted by giant wings. He landed in a heap. When he scrambled back to his feet, blood trickled from a cut above his eye.

Anari stomped and wheeled, gathering strength from Lord Crow's war blessing. A surge of power raised the small hairs on the back of his arms.

Kayin tried to attack again, limping. Again Anari knocked him back without touching him.

This time, Kayin didn't try to attack with his sword or ax. He knelt and shrieked to invoke Lord Raven's war blessing.

Anari heard the rustle of invisible feathers. The sky was blue and clear, but the air smelled like lightning.

Kayin rose to his feet and began his dance.

Anari drew his dagger with his left hand. With a scream, he brought it down like a striking beak. He imagined the beak piercing Kayin's weapon arm. A rush of shadow flew at Kayin.

Kayin flinched. Fresh blood dripped from his sleeve. His sword slipped from his fingers and clattered to the ground, but he did not concede defeat. He swung his good arm in a wing strike.

Anari shifted the curve of his dance, raising his elbow like a bird sheltering behind its wing. He felt only a breeze.

Kayin dropped his arms and abandoned his dance.

Victory tasted like blood in Anari's mouth.

The Fox priest stepped forward and raised the beaded crown. "We have witnessed the strength of the heirs' connection to the gods. The challenge is over and—"

"No!" Kayin shouted. "I do not concede!"

Kayin's favored arm hung useless by his side. He reached for his ax with his other hand and drew it after a few moments of fumbling.

Lord Crow's war blessing still surged through Anari. Anari curved his arms, preparing to use a wing of wind to knock aside any attack.

Kayin dropped to sit in the dirt. He raised his ax high and brought it down with an all-too-human scream. The wet crunch of the ax severing his foot carried clearly. Blood streamed across the ground.

Shadow wings stretched under Kayin's arms. He lifted his good arm and the shadows leapt from the ground and took to the sky like a dense flight of ravens. He dropped his arm and they dove at Anari, led by the real raven who accompanied Kayin.

Anari tried to knock the shadow ravens away like he had Kayin's earlier attacks, but they sliced through his defense like the air it was made out of.

The moment before they struck him, he threw up his arm to protect his eyes and curled into a ball on the ground. The sound of wings battered him. Talons tore his flesh and yanked out clumps of his hair. The pain continued after the attack stopped, burning through him like a fever that would only end in death.

Anari lowered his arm only enough to peer over it with the eye Lord Crow had given him. He remembered the pain of a crow's beak piercing his eye deeply enough to scrape the socket, remembered it too well to risk his remaining good eye.

The shadow ravens rose above Kayin in a huge cloud. Anari saw the outlines of the mango trees through their transparent wings. They looked like shadows, but the bleeding gouges in his flesh were real. They'd ripped away his helmet and cut through his armor. Thanks to Lord Crow's gift, he could see the vulnerable spots the ravens had targeted. The next wave would open his flesh to the bone. His lifeblood would spill across the challenge ground.

Without healing, Kayin wouldn't outlast him by

much. Anari could see his heart fluttering far too rapidly inside his rib cage, pumping his blood away. A carrion mask hung over him as he raised his arm to signal another strike.

An audience of the dead had replaced the witnesses of the Eight Houses. Ranks of corpses killed in battle circled the challenge ground. They waited for Anari to join them. They watched with empty eye sockets, ignoring the wounds that had killed them. One of the dead seemed to stare directly at Anari.

Her skeleton was small, almost delicate. A red gash hung over her throat like a necklace. Her fingers curved into claws, as if she fought to hold herself back. The familiarity of the gesture jarred Anari.

He ignored the risk to his good eye and lowered his arm all the way. Pain speared through his head as his doubled vision sprang back. Worse was the shock that echoed through him as the corpses revealed themselves to be, not an audience of the dead, but the witnesses from the Eight Houses. Death masked them all. His mother stared at him with love and fear for him, her clever fingers crooked into claws. Her death wound floated above her throat.

Anari heard Calogero's voice in memory. "The war will go on until we are all dead, of plague or battle, but my people will not go alone."

It didn't matter who became oba. Everyone Anari cared about would die. All because Lord Rat protected the Eight Houses from plague-infested rats, and the infidels wouldn't believe that reason even if anyone told them.

Kayin brought his arm sweeping down. The shadow ravens dove to strike.

"Lord Crow, I claim my favor!" Anari shouted.

Lord Crow appeared in front of Anari, holding a wedge of golden-green mango. The shadow ravens hung motionless in the air, mid-attack.

Kayin didn't blink. Or breathe. Or move.

Nothing did. Not a single glossy leaf rustled in the breeze, because there was no breeze.

Lord Crow bit the mango's glistening orange flesh and slurped it into his mouth as juices trickled between his fingers. "Perfect."

"Are they—?"

"They will be fine." Lord Crow cast an assessing glance at the statue-like crowd. "For now. I thought we could use some privacy for this discussion. You *are* going to claim your favor, yes?"

Anari collected himself. "Lord Crow," he said, "I ask a large favor of you, but I beg you to consider it, by the eye that I lost and by Virtue Two: Collecting the Precious."

"Tell me of this favor."

"I ask you to take the Scorned under your wing and to let them use their skills in your service," Anari said baldly. He braced himself.

When Lord Crow did not immediately strike him down, Anari pressed on. "I was taught to see value where others do not, as is the way of the Crow. It shames me that I was blind to the virtues of the Scorned. These people are valuable. They have talents that House Crow could use. I did not change when I fled Ayeli Asatsvyi, yet the Scorned were the only ones who saw that I was not worthless, despite my lack of a Band tattoo."

"You are certain that this is how you want to use your favor? You don't want the power to destroy your enemy? You don't want to be oba?"

Anari looked at Kayin. He wore the impassive expression of a warrior determined to hide any weakness, but taut lines of pain etched his face. His unseeing eyes glared into nothing.

Anari glanced at where Adetosoye sat among the witnesses from House Raven. He hunched forward on his stool, his arms braced against his knees like the last support beams of a collapsing house.

"Kayin is not my enemy. We want the same thing." Anari returned his gaze to Lord Crow. "I ask you to take the Scorned under your wing, by virtue of—"

"Yes, yes," interrupted Lord Crow. "Just these ones?"

Anari didn't allow himself to smile, but he felt like it despite the pain he was in. Lord Crow was intrigued. "No," Anari answered. "I ask that you take all current Scorned ones under your wing. Do you agree?"

Lord Crow cocked his head and surveyed Anari. Anari felt beads of sweat forming at his hairline.

"That is too many," Lord Crow said.

"All the Scorned currently in Ayeli Asatsvyi," Anari countered. "Let the other Scorned ones apply for your sanction, along with those already under your wing who want a child."

"You cannot use this for yourself. You will go into exile. If you return, you will become Scorned but *you* can never be accepted back into the Eight Houses."

"I understand." Anari hadn't allowed the kernel of hope to grow, but it still hurt.

"All the Scorned currently in Ayeli Asatsvyi is a large number of people," Lord Crow said. "The other gods will be angry at how fast my strength grows." He grinned and shrugged. "I have no choice; I have to grant you a favor. They cannot argue that this isn't within my domain. I even bargained you down from your first demand."

Anari snatched a glance at the crowd of motionless witnesses. The marks of their deaths were fading. It was working. "You agree, then? You will grant my favor?" he pressed.

Lord Crow's eyes gleamed. "Yes, I will." He tapped his finger against his teeth. "What shall we name this new Band? It must be a bird, and not a hunter ... I have it! Band Finch." He surveyed the motley assemblage before him. "Finch is a very small god, with no worshipers, but he will enjoy growing. I hereby grant your favor."

Lord Crow flicked his hand and sent Kayin's ravens wheeling up into the sky like so many translucent kites.

Shadows swept around Lord Crow. Anari heard the clap of a pair of giant wings. He felt Lord Crow's favor tear its way out from under his skin. He gasped in pain.

The crowd echoed his gasp as they stirred to life. They stared up at the transparent ravens wheeling in the sky. Anari realized that to their eyes, the ravens had been about to attack when they blinked out of existence and reappeared far above.

Anari looked hard at the witnesses from the Eight Houses. He no longer saw them blemished by the spectre of their approaching doom. Only Adetosoye still wore his death. One more thing was needed to banish that.

"I concede!" Anari called out. "I accept exile."

Confusion cracked Kayin's mask of warriorlike impassivity. "What?"

"I concede," Anari repeated.

A wave of prickly heat swept over him. His legs felt weak. He swayed. A knot of pain tightened his belly. He sat down abruptly.

"I accept your concession." Kayin drew a deep breath. "I am oba!" he shouted. "Let all the gods and Houses witness."

"We witness," answered the watching crowd.

The Fox priest carried the beaded crown to Kayin, and a priest from House Raven hurried to his side to heal him.

Kayin put up a hand to fend them off. "Bring Adetosoye to me," he insisted. "I must be touching him when the cascade flows through me."

Sitting upright was too difficult. Anari eased himself down to lie on his back. The sky was bright blue and clear of clouds.

Calogero appeared above him. His eyes glittered fever-bright. "Marking me once wasn't enough for you?" he challenged Anari. He brandished his uninjured hand. A fresh Band tattoo of a finch adorned it. "What have you done?"

Romesh shouldered him roughly aside and knelt next to Anari. "Hold on, Anari. Soon I will be able to heal you. You only need to hold on for a little bit longer. Lay still and try not to move."

Anari grabbed Romesh's sleeve. "Heal him first." He indicated Calogero. "You have to heal him first. Without him, it will all be for nothing. Promise me!"

Romesh scowled. "Very well. Now lay still!"

"What have you done?" Calogero demanded again.

Anari smiled. "I protected us all."

Calogero's horrified face was the last thing Anari saw before the world slid sideways and disappeared.

8

ANARI OPENED HIS eyes to see a familiar mural of lilies and lotus flowers above him. He lay in his bed. The golden light of dawn poured through his window, gilding everything it touched.

An extraordinary sense of health and well-being fizzed through him. He sat up and laughed out loud at how quick and easy the movement was. He spread his arms and stretched, savoring the feeling of soft cloth against clean skin. He waited for pain to return, but it didn't.

The sound of wings captured his attention. He stared at his window, where a crow perched on the sill.

"Checking on me for Lord Crow, are you?" Anari asked.

The crow declined to answer. It turned its head to the side and stared at him with one beady eye.

"You can tell him I am good. I haven't felt this well in a very long time." Anari laughed again.

The door swung open. One of the oba's guards held it. Anari glimpsed a crowd in the hallway beyond. None of them rose to enter his room. When he heard the *thump* step *thump* step rhythm of someone approaching on crutches, Anari understood why.

The strings of beads hanging from the oba's crown swung back and forth as Kayin propelled himself into the room. He braced himself on one crutch as he pushed the door shut.

Anari gestured to a bench. "Please, sit down. You must be tired from learning how to walk with those."

Kayin swung himself onto the bench and leaned his crutches against the wall. "They tell me I'll get used to it. Once the scars aren't as tender, I can have a wooden leg made. Then I may be able to walk with only a cane."

After they shook hands in greeting, Anari waited for Kayin to tell him why he was here.

"Many people want to speak to you before you go into exile," Kayin said. "I insisted on being first. One of the privileges of rulership."

"You paid the price for it."

Kayin leaned forward to speak, but he overbalanced and had to grab the side of the bench to keep from falling. "I paid a price," he said. "But you paid one too."

Anari's hand flew to his face. In his burst of wellbeing, he had forgotten about his Crow eye. The world looked normal. "It's still—?"

"Yes. You still bear the mark of how much Lord Crow favors you." Kayin paused. "You spoke with the god during our combat, didn't you? The Scorned—"

"They are not Scorned any more," Anari interrupted.

"The new members of Band Finch, then. They say that Lord Crow owed you a favor. You could have used it to win. Instead, you brought Scorned ones into your

House. Why?"

"Do you remember when your guide-father found us fighting over the sling?"

Kayin's expression smoothed to impassivity. "Yes."

"Yesterday—it *was* yesterday?"

Kayin nodded.

"Yesterday, you and I made different decisions," Anari said. "But we did it for the same reason. We both protected our people. I couldn't have done that if I used my favor to become oba."

"Adetosoye knew there would be great differences between us, but I doubt he imagined this."

"How is he? Were you able to heal him during the cascade?"

Real happiness touched Kayin's expression for the first time. "Yes. He is completely healed. This morning, he ate a full plate of yams with red stew and called for more."

"It was worth it for you, then."

Kayin nodded. "It is worth it, although there are those who will say that you would have been a better oba than I am."

"If you are as dedicated to protecting all the people who are now yours as you were to protecting your guide-father, you will be a great oba."

Kayin leaned forward cautiously. This time he did not overbalance. "I want you to know that I will care for your mother as a son, though she is of House Crow and I am—" He faltered. "And I am beyond House allegiances."

"Thank you. I know she will be safe under your wing."

Kayin braced himself against the bench and stood. He balanced on one leg as he positioned his crutches.

"She's waiting to speak to you, along with a crowd of other people, including that ragtag flock of new Crows. I'll send her in next."

The crow in the window stretched out a wing and began to preen itself, ignoring them, as if it were dismissing the oba.

Anari's mother rushed in, threw her arms around him without a word, and held him tight. He rested his cheek on top of her head.

She finally released him and stepped back. "I was so worried about you!" she exclaimed. "The Crow chief healer at the battlefront sent word that you'd never arrived. You disappeared! And then you came back and instead of conceding without a fight, you challenged for the beaded crown." She smacked him lightly. "You weren't supposed to do that!"

He smiled. "I was worried about you, too."

"And why are you grinning at me? You have to go into exile now. At least you will be over the mountains and away from the war, but you will be living among the Scorned. Anything could happen."

Anari took a deep breath. "I'm not going over the mountains. I plan on crossing the desert land bridge and living among our enemies."

She gasped. "But the war! They will kill you. Why would you do such a thing?"

He studied her carefully, with both his human eye and his Crow one. To both eyes, she overflowed with health and vitality. "I believe the war will end soon," he told her. "I need to build a new life for myself, and I think that's the right place for me."

He hoped he would have Calogero's help, once he explained things to the diplomat who had been a Scorned foreigner and was now among the newest members of House Crow.

"Whatever you are thinking, my son, remember the Third Temptation of the Crow. Don't fall in love with your own cleverness." She studied him. "You are still grinning," she observed tartly. "Didn't you listen to anything I said?"

"I did. I'm happy because I know you will be fine."

She huffed, but it was an affectionately fussy sound with no real anger behind it. "Since we've established that we will both be fine, I'll let you speak to the others who are waiting."

She opened the door and paused.

Anari waited for her to speak, until he realized that she was not breathing. Her stillness was not her choice, but that of a god.

Feathers rustled behind him.

Anari spun to see the crow in his window launching itself into his room. Mid-flight, it exploded into a cloud of feathers.

Anari dropped to his knees and bowed his head. The feet of a god in human form appeared in front of him.

"Why is that?" Lord Crow demanded. "Why do you know that she will be fine? You saw her death at the challenge, as clearly as I did. The stink of carrion hung over the whole crowd. Now it is gone. Why?"

Anari dared to look up. "I did not know you were here with us, Lord Crow."

"You never know for certain when the gods are watching," Lord Crow said. One of his eyelids shivered in what might have been a wink. "Answer my question."

"You agreed to take the Scorned under your wing."

"Yes." Lord Crow bobbed his head.

Now came the tricky bit. "And to let them use their

skills," Anari reminded him.

"And to let them use their skills in my service," Lord Crow agreed.

"You should know those that you have accepted," Anari said. He pointed through the open doorway at the individual Scorned ones waiting in the hall. "Rasee is a deckhand. Galilahi does fine piecework. Jian is a master carver. Calogero has a silver tongue worthy of the best speaker in Band Nightingale. He was an infidel, and therefore a Scorned one, when he was sent here as an ambassador—"

Lord Crow froze. His eyes fixed on Anari as though he were contemplating a particularly juicy snail. "An infidel!" he shouted. "You tricked me. Nobody tricks *me*!"

Anari felt the cold wind of shadow wings sweeping toward him.

"Not you!" he cried. "The trick is not on you!"

Lord Crow's eyes narrowed. "Explain."

"This favor will increase your strength. It will help your people." Anari hoped that the Book of Crow was accurate about how much Lord Crow enjoyed plaguing those who saw him as an upstart godling, a Band god who could not manage a House. "And it will greatly annoy the other House gods."

"Why do you think I would choose to annoy the other gods?"

"You have no choice. You granted me the favor. And this will help all our people. If Calogero uses his skills under your wing, he will be our first ambassador to the infidels," Anari said, speaking so rapidly that he stumbled over his words. "He will cross the desert and return to his country as *your* representative. Lord Rat will be required to make certain that the rats where

Calogero may go do not carry plague. As a diplomat, Calogero will need to be able to travel anywhere in the country that he is posted to, and so Lord Raven will lose the battlefields he revels in."

"How?" Lord Crow demanded.

"The infidels only fight because they think that we hide the cure for the plague from them. They are desperate. End the plague, and we end the war."

Lord Crow threw back his head and cawed with laughter. "What a wonderful trick on Lord Raven. And clearly it was not I who planned it. I look forward to telling Lord Rat that he must soon depart to cleanse an entire country. Well done."

Anari was left uncertain who had tricked whom, but at least the favor Lord Crow owed him had been settled. The Eight Houses wouldn't be destroyed by a pointless war. The loss of his eye was worth it.

Lord Crow spread his shadow wings to leave.

"Lord Crow, wait!" Anari called. "The challenge is over. What will happen to the Crow eye you granted me?"

"Keep it, for now. You may find its abilities useful."

Anari frowned. "What do you mean?" He did not want to see more death.

Lord Crow cocked his head to the side. "Did you think you could trick the gods and then quietly retire to exile?"

"… Yes?"

Lord Crow laughed. "Then you tricked yourself, too. You may have won your peace, but this is not the end."

WANT MORE?

Good news: Yes, there will be another book in this novella series!
Bad news: It may take a while to be released.

Go to the author's book page for *The Unkindness of Ravens* to find updates, publication timelines, and recommendations for African- and Indian-influenced fantasy by other authors that you may enjoy:

http://www.aswiebe.com/moreunkindness.html

For author news and free fiction, join the author's newsletter at **www.aswiebe.com**.

ALSO BY ABRA STAFFIN-WIEBE

Shorter Works

"Ekaterina and the Firebird," published by Tor.com and available at all major ebook retailers

Go to **http://www.aswiebe.com/** to discover all the worlds of her short fiction, which has appeared in publications including *Tor.com*, *Escape Pod*, and *Odyssey Magazine*.

Writing as Abra S.W.

A Circus of Brass and Bone

Keep reading for a taste of something completely different!

A CIRCUS OF BRASS AND BONE

A Circus of Brass and Bone is a post-apocalyptic steampunk novel about a circus traveling through the collapse of civilization after a catastrophic aetheric chain-reaction. People must come together or die. Find out where *A Circus of Brass and Bone* is available to purchase at http://www.aswiebe.com/morecircus.html.

EXCERPT

William McCormick
Boston, Massachusetts

"Hello, can somebody help?" William called. "Please, my mother is trapped! Is anybody there?"

He held his breath. Soft whimpers and moans came from the wounded in the factory behind him. As if in answer, he heard a man shouting, "Help! Help me!" He sounded nearby.

A man grown might be strong enough to move the table pinning William's mother. He was strong enough to shout; maybe he wasn't hurt too bad. If William helped him, he could help William's mother.

William let go of the door frame and stood on his own. He swayed a bit, but didn't fall. He took a step. So far, so good. If he had to, he would crawl to get help for his mother—but he'd rather walk.

By taking it slow and stopping often to lean against a light post or a doorway, William made it two blocks. "Oh, bless you! May the sun shine upon you!" he heard.

William peered around the corner. One man lay trapped beneath the wreckage of a cart and the mound of coal it had carried. The dead carthorse lay beside him. A group of about ten rough-looking men worked together to free him, under the direction of a large man with a jaunty hat that sat oddly with his stained workman's clothes. They were hard men, William's da would have said, but then, his da looked a hard man himself, when he came back from building canals. He only softened up when he'd spent some time around William's mam.

Two of the men pulled out the splintered planks that used to be a cart. The rest shifted the mound of coal. Some carried it away in their hands or their hats. Others used pieces of wreckage to clear a large swathe away. They were *helping*.

William lurked near the corner, watching, as he tried to figure out the best way to introduce himself. When the rough-looking men pulled a particularly large piece of wreckage out, the fallen man gasped and winced. The man with the hat squatted beside him.

"Are you alright there?" asked the man with the hat. "It'll be over soon. Tell me, stranger, what's your name?"

"Conrad Zero," the trapped man gasped.

"Zero? What kind of name is that for a man?"

"At immigration, they asked my name. When I hesitated too long—not sure if I wanted to give my full name, you see, in case trouble tried to follow me here—the official shrugged and wrote, 'Zero'. Suits me well enough. A new life, a new start, a new name." He looked down at the debris covering him. "If I get out of here."

"I'm Chad Valentine," the man with the hat said, "and we'll be getting you out."

"Call him Valentine," chorused the other men.

"It's 'cause he's such a sweetheart of a slave driver," one of the men added.

"It's not like we'll be going back to canal-building, Tommy-boy," Valentine said. "Not after this."

"No," Tommy-boy agreed, looking around. "It'll be building the factories back up for us."

"Maybe. Then again, maybe not." A smile William didn't understand crossed Valentine's lips. He looked back over his shoulder at where William lurked. "And what's your name, boy? Come on out, don't be shy."

William eased around the corner. Nerves made him want to fiddle with something, so he stuck his hands in his pockets.

"William McCormick, sir. My mam's hurt. Will you help her, please?"

Valentine puffed up his chest. "Sure and we will! Where is she?"

"The crystal factory, sir."

"A factory full of womenfolk needing help, you say? How about it, lads?"

A chorus of approval came from the group.

William smiled, glad they'd help but a little uncomfortable.

"Let's just get Conrad out, and then we'll be along to help your mam." Valentine studied the reduced weight of the coal on top of the man. "Conrad, we'll grab your arms and pull you out. Holler if you feel something shifting in a real bad way."

Valentine and Tommy each took an arm and

heaved. Conrad yelped and hissed between his teeth, but he didn't tell them to stop. He popped out like a chimney sweep from a smokestack, his clothing rags, covered in coal dust from neck to toe.

"Much obliged!" he said.

"Now, a prosperous businessman like yourself will be wanting to repay those who helped you, surely?" Valentine asked. His gang stepped closer.

"Oh, aye," Conrad agreed sourly, "and I just happen to have the monies from the coal I've sold so far here in my pocket."

"Would never have occurred to me," Valentine said blandly.

Conrad winced. "Agh, but I feel like I've got ants biting all over me!" He bent and swatted at his trousers, sending a cloud of black dust up into the air. When he straightened, he swayed. He grabbed ahold of Tommy to steady himself.

Tommy tensed and his hand knotted. As quickly, he relaxed, but not before William saw.

William edged back a bit. "Mr. Valentine, sir, can you help my mam?"

"Lead the way, kid!" Valentine said, counting the coins Conrad had handed him and passing a few along to his friends.

The men laughed and patted each other on the back, their spirits raised by the successful rescue. Conrad shrugged and followed along. When William led them along and they passed those lying in the street, dead or struggling to push themselves up, the men grew quieter. When they entered the factory, they were utterly silent as they took in what had happened in the crystal workshop.

William's vision had recovered from the blinding

effect of the flash of light. He could see clearly now. He wished he couldn't. Most of the women and children laboring in the workshop looked like they'd died painfully, if quickly. Their bodies had contorted beyond the tolerance of muscle and bone. Blood congealed in their eyes. He'd seen it before, when he'd crawled to his mam, but not—not all at once, like. Some hadn't died from the storm. Flying bricks from the wall had done for two more. Crystal shards pincushioned half-a-dozen others. Children lay in pools of their life's blood, their faces cut beyond recognition by crystal prisms that had exploded at precisely child-height.

"They were just kids," said Patrick Sullivan, one of the younger men in Valentine's mob.

One of the small bleeding bodies stirred. Patrick jumped forward to help. "Here now, we'll get you to a doctor—"

The child gave a last convulsive shudder and then—stopped. A fly straggled in from outside and landed on the body. It scuttled around, its suckered tongue tasting dried sweat and blood.

Patrick turned to the side, braced himself against the wall, and vomited a chunky spew that splashed when it struck the ground. It looked like he'd eaten stew, William thought. He felt shaky and cold. His mam cooked up a good stew.

Sensing richer reward, the fly buzzed up and flew over to investigate. That made William wonder: why weren't there more flies? It was a terrible thought, but it nagged at him.

"William …"

The whispery voice of his mam fetched him across the room so fast he didn't remember anything between here and there.

"Praise be, one still lives," Valentine said in a subdued voice. Louder: "Come along, lads!"

Even the new rescuee, Conrad, charged forward and helped to lift the heavy worktable away. He winced a couple of times, but he didn't slack and he didn't complain.

William danced impatiently from foot to foot. As soon as the men heaved the worktable to the side, he darted in and clutched his mam's hand.

"How do you feel?" he asked.

"Better. I can breathe. But—ah!—it still hurts."

"William," Valentine said, "I know a doc who'll fix your mam up. The doc lives not too far from here, near the edge of the rich district." He didn't add, *If he's still alive*, but he didn't have to. "We can go and bring the doctor back to your mam."

Fear of being left alone with the dead and dying gripped William. What if they didn't come back? Something of the same feeling must have touched his mam, for she said, "I can walk, I think. With help."

Valentine said, "Could be I saw something that might help."

He left and returned with a wooden pole cut down to the right size for a walking staff. A minute's quick work with his knife rounded the top into a knob that wouldn't hurt to rest weight on.

"And why would a man like you happen to have noticed a fine *shillelagh* like that?" William's mam asked, a touch of humor in her voice despite everything.

A blush tinged Valentine's ears. For a moment, he looked much less like a hard man.

They levered William's mam to her feet and braced her when she swayed. With the staff under her hand,

Valentine holding her elbow, and William hovering nearby, she hobbled unsteadily to the door. Patrick went ahead of them, clearing obstructions away so she wouldn't trip and fall. Some obstructions he moved more gently than others.

Out on the street, William looked around with newly clear eyes. The few folk who had been struggling to push themselves up now swayed on their feet. One man clutched his arm to his side; it hung at an unnatural angle.

William tugged at Valentine's sleeve. "Can he come, too?"

"Very well," Valentine said magnanimously. He paused near the injured man. "We're going along to the doctor. You may have a walk with us, if you like."

Desperate gratitude filled the man's face. "Aye, I will! Blessings on you." He fell into line behind them.

The others swayed in place, their eyes still shocked and dazed. William remembered the horrible clutch of fear he'd felt at the idea of being left alone. He shouted, "You lot can keep company with us."

Valentine looked down on him, a peculiar expression on his face. "Can they, then? Well." He raised his voice and added, "*If* you help along those with trouble."

Most roused and stumbled along, helping each other when it was needed.

One man remained. "I—I have to find my wife," he said.

William looked down at his feet to avoid seeing the man's desperate, hoping expression.

A dead fly curled on the ground. Two feet away, there was another one. A cluster of sparrows sprawled on their backs near a wall, feathers ruffled in death, twiglike legs bent and twisted.

They walked on.

Corpses salted the streets: men, women, children, horses, dogs, cats, rats, birds, and even insects. No living thing that moved upon the earth had been spared.

Survivors sat on stoops or clung to the doorways of shops and factories. William wondered what awaited inside. He didn't go look. None of Valentine's mob did; they clung close together and stuck to the center of the street. They called out to the other survivors, though, offering help and inviting them along.

The survivors would look up, staring at them with haunted eyes.

Did you see—? those eyes would ask.

Yes, yes, I did, their eyes answered.

Some of them would follow. The mob doubled and then tripled in size. A carthorse that had outlived its master trotted alongside them, and skittish dogs trailed in their shadow.

Valentine looked down at William with a wry twist to his mouth, as if to say, "See what you started?"

William lifted his chin. His mam watched. What else could he have done?

When they reached the doctor's house, on the outskirts of Beacon Hill, Valentine waved the crowd to silence and knocked on the door. After a wait long enough to be worrying, William heard the snick of a lock being turned.

A disheveled lady opened the door, got one look at the small mob following in Valentine's wake, and slammed it shut again. Patrick started forward with an angry look on his face, but Valentine waved him back.

Making his case to the door, he wheedled, "Ach, Elizabeth, it's your old friend Valentine. You wouldna turn away a friend on such a grim day? And the boy beside me with his injured mother?"

The door creaked open. The lady had taken the opportunity to twist her black hair up into a bun, perch spectacles on her nose, and cover her dress with an apron starched stiff enough to repel a sea of blood. She glared at Valentine over her spectacles, her dark brows set in an unyielding line. "I only have room for the wounded inside. The rest of your ducklings can wait. And to you, my name is Dr. Fallon."

Dead silence greeted her. "What—?" Patrick began, with an expression like a stunned ox. A sharp elbow to the ribs from Valentine silenced him.

Relenting somewhat, Dr. Fallon added, "Your lads can put the kettle on the hob and make tea for the rest of the lot. With sugar, whether they like it or not. Might have to wait their turn for a teacup."

She strode back into the house, not looking back to see if any followed.

In an undertone, Valentine hissed to Patrick, "Keep yer gob shut! Did you think a high-and-mighty doctor with his choice of patients would tend to Irish rabble? Lizzie's worked harder to prove herself than any man among us. She's a mighty fine doctor, too. Don't call her Lizzie, though, or she'll tear a strip out of your hide. Now go on and make tea!"

Valentine assisted William's mam into the house. She made little noises that might, William worried, be a sign of pain—but sounded more like a suppressed case of the giggles.

Dr. Fallon's parlor had been converted into a patient examination room. Valentine and William got her into the room and settled according to the doctor's instructions.

"Valentine—" Dr. Fallon began.

"Ah, it fair gladdened my heart to see you standing there when we opened the door!" he interrupted. "So many dead, I feared you'd be among them."

Dr. Fallon seemed immune to Valentine's heart-gladdening. "I was down in the cellar, preparing solutions, when the storm hit. My lights went out. I heard the most terrible sound, like hundreds of voices screaming. Then a convulsive fit struck me. I had just recovered when you arrived. Now, Valentine, go on out—I have a patient to see to, and I think she'd like her privacy for the exam."

The tips of Valentine's ears turned red, and he bowed himself out. William stayed.

William helped Dr. Fallon move his mother. The doctor listened to her breathing, had her spit in a cup, asked questions, and gently probed to find where the pain was.

"Your chances are good," Dr. Fallon said, finally. "That worktable broke some ribs, but there's no blood in your spit, and I don't hear any fluid gurgling when you breathe. That means the ribs didn't puncture your lungs. Your abdomen isn't stiff, so you may be lucky enough to not have internal bleeding. I'd give you a shot of bone aether to speed healing, but all my vials shattered when that—that ungodly whatever-it-was struck. Keep breathing normally, stay abed for a week and then go very slow for the next five. Wrap your ribs before you go about your day. Your boy here can help you with that. And don't lift anything!"

William's mam smiled weakly. "I'm not even a bit tempted."

Dr. Fallon barked a laugh. "You're more sensible than most of my male patients!"

William helped his mother to sit in an overstuffed chair in the entranceway and then came back in to watch. His sense of propriety no longer threatened, Valentine did as well. Dr. Fallon was less gentle with her next patient.

"There's nothing wrong with you that a good scrubbing won't take care of," Dr. Fallon told Conrad. "Bathe with soap, until you're clean all over, or those cuts and scrapes will get infected. With all this commotion," she said disapprovingly, "the bath houses are probably closed. Bathe in a barrel of water if you have to, but get the coal dust and filth off. Then apply this liniment and bandages."

"Barrel it is," Conrad said gloomily. "Not like I have a fancy bathtub like those highfalutin rich folk with their indoor running water and all."

Valentine leaned forward, and his eyes gleamed. "Says who? Think on it, man. How many died? Did you think the rich were spared? If we go knocking on doors, we'll find one where nobody answers. And then—" He laughed, leaning back. "Then you'll have your bath!"

Dr. Fallon didn't look shocked, and she didn't tell Valentine that what he was thinking was wrong, William noticed. Maybe she wasn't too fond of her neighbors, either.

"Ten blocks up, there's a fine blue and white mansion with hydrangeas growing in front. The owner rushes to the physician when any member of his family so much as sneezes. I'm only a poor substitute when his regular physician isn't available, of course—" she cut a length of bandage off the roll with a vicious snip, "—but under the circumstances, I doubt he would have been able to reach his regular physician. I haven't heard from him, which makes me think that neither he nor his household is up to repelling visitors."

"Bless you, doctor!"

She snorted. "Get those who need medical care organized before you leave, with able-bodied men to help them."

"I will that!"

"Leave?" William asked, but nobody answered him.

William trailed after Valentine as he left the doctor's parlor. Valentine was as good as his word. He got volunteers to help the injured, checked to see that they'd all had sweet tea, shook hands, and patted backs.

William followed. He saw how heads turned after them, how dull, stunned faces regained a semblance of life when they passed.

William stayed hot on Valentine's heels as he rounded the corner of the house. His work gang loitered there, waiting. "Come on, lads!" he said.

"You can't just leave them!" William burst out.

"I'm not one of the saints, lad, to be watching out for all in need!" William felt his face fall. Valentine hastily added, "But that's not what I'm doing at all! Just—looking about a bit. You should go and tend to your mam."

"She's resting here as well as she can. Where could I take her? Back to the North End? You think she'll get better care there? You think maybe this only hurt the rich folk? I'm coming along with you, I am."

Or you might not come back.

A trace of a scowl lingering on his lips, Valentine led the others off at a pace brisk enough that William had to trot to keep up.

When he saw the house Dr. Fallon had

recommended, however, Valentine seemed to forget his irritation. "Now, lads, isn't that there better than living all crowded together in a one-room apartment with your friends who fart in their sleep and never wash their socks?"

A roar of agreement went up from the half-dozen men following him. William couldn't help but shout along. He and his mam shared an apartment with another family, and the youngest boy had a digestion that cabbage disagreed with. William himself, of course, never offended.

He tilted his head back and stared up at the big house. Blue and white, yes, but that was like describing a castle as "greyish." Gingerbread trim curlicued around the house. Turrets jutted from the roof. Perfect for a boy to guard over the house from, he couldn't help thinking. Large bay windows opened up onto the lawn, and he imagined curling up in the sunlight with a schoolbook, as he thought a boy who lived in this house would. *That* boy would still be in school, not trudging all over town trying to find any job that would take him.

Envy spiked through William.

Valentine jerked the bell pull. A bell rang inside the house, but no footsteps answered it. They waited long enough for a maid to reach the door. They waited long enough for the mistress of the house to rouse herself and answer the door if the maid could not. They waited even a bit longer than that.

Valentine opened the door a crack. No irate butler appeared to chase them out. Valentine pushed the door open wider and strode inside.

William timidly followed. Over the threshold, he stopped and gaped. Only the grumbled curses of the men piling up behind him propelled him into the house. Polished wood gleamed, oak and mahogany carved so artfully that William thought they belonged in a museum. He wouldn't dare sit on one of the fancy chairs in case he messed it up, even though his legs still ached. They looked awful inviting, though, all overstuffed plush and brocade.

A hunting landscape papered the hall, dogs baying happily after a fox while figures on horseback watched from a distant hill. Birds flew through blue skies near the ceiling. The poppies and daisies painted at the bottom stood out sharp and vivid, as if they sprouted from the baseboards; William felt an impulse to stoop and pick one. A grand open staircase swept up from the entryway to the second floor.

It seemed so fantastic, like something from a dream or a storybook. They could live here now, he and his mam, if they wanted to. William tilted back his head, a huge smile on his face, and saw—a gas-lit chandelier. It hung above their heads like the Sword of Damocles. Sunlight glittered on brass. Broken rainbows danced across their faces.

Fragments of memory. Flesh cut to ribbons. Small bodies. The cries of the dying.

William bolted outside and vomited in the hydrangeas. Valentine followed him out and patted him awkwardly on the shoulder. "It's all right, boy. Bad things take some men like that. They'll be strong as long as they need to be, and then ... Everything will be fine now."

William looked up at him and didn't believe a word he said. But he went back in, though he avoided looking at the chandelier, afraid of what he might see reflected in its prisms.

Valentine's men spread out to explore their new domain.

Two rampaged upstairs. "I'm sleeping on a feather bed tonight!" Tommy hollered.

Patrick said, "I'm going to eat like a rich man!" The others scoffed and asked him if he'd be cooking up this rich food himself, but that didn't stop him from going in search of the kitchen.

The joyful shouts upstairs stopped abruptly, and the men came back to stand above the staircase, grim-faced. "We found the nursery," Tommy said. "And the master's study," the other added.

Patrick returned from the kitchen looking as if he'd lost his appetite. "The butler, the maid, the footman, and the cook were all in the kitchen when the storm hit. I think the cook would have lived if she hadn't collapsed onto the range."

Valentine winced. "That's not pork for dinner I was smelling, then." He pointed at William. "You stay here. We'll need to haul them out."

"Bury them, you mean?" William asked.

Valentine hesitated. "Of course, of course. In the garden. That'll be nice for them, won't it? Like sleeping under flowers."

"I know they're dead," William told him. "I'm not a baby."

"That you're not," Valentine said dryly. "More like a bird chirping in my ear."

William stayed.

Valentine's gang went up the curving staircase. There was thumping, and some cursing, and then they came down the stairs with carefully sheet-wrapped bundles, some pitifully small. They went out back. The *thunk* of shovel hitting dirt carried into the entryway, but William stayed where he was. More cursing. When silence fell, William went out into the back garden.

The men stood, hats in hand, around a large, churned-up patch of ground. Seven new mounds lay at the foot of the rose bushes, but what had been planted would not blossom into life next spring. Valentine mumbled the Lord's prayer and they all trouped back inside.

"Rich folk like these will have their own indoor water closet," Patrick said. "Did anyone see it? I'd like to wash the grave dirt from under my fingernails." One of the others pointed him in the right direction. After a few moments, he came back looking disgusted. "I thought I'd like using one of those fancy water closets, but the water wasn't running at all! I used a pitcher and basin to wash my hands, just like usual."

"Was there a bathtub?" Conrad asked.

"Aye and there was, but likely it won't be working!"

"I'll just be seeing about that!" Conrad said. "Even if I still need to haul the water, I'll be having a bath in a proper bathtub! Just like *I* was a rich man!"

He darted off, and after a moment, the sound of trickling water came to their ears. "I left the tap open, and there came a few drops. Now it's a proper stream, it is!" he shouted down.

Patrick scowled.

Valentine laughed. "Lads, I found something a mite more important than water: the liquor cabinet. It'll be a proper wake!"

That roused the spirits of the men and they happily followed Valentine. William trailed along, though his mam didn't let him drink anything stronger than short beer.

"Here's to the man of the house and his generous

stock of liquor!" Valentine said, lifting a glass of whiskey.

William thought of the folk lying under a thin blanket of dirt in the garden, and he couldn't smile.

Valentine looked William's way, and his smile faded a bit. "May God and the angels welcome him and his family, and Mary intercede—"

A horrible gurgling scream interrupted the toast.

END OF EXCERPT

To keep reading, get a copy of *A Circus of Brass and Bone* by Abra S.W. Find out where it's available at **http://www.aswiebe.com/morecircus.html**.

ABOUT THE AUTHOR

Abra Staffin-Wiebe loves dark science fiction, cheerful horror, and futuristic fairy tales. Dozens of her short stories have appeared at publications including *Tor.com*, *F&SF*, *Escape Pod*, and *Odyssey Magazine*. She's a third-culture kid who grew up in places including India and Central Africa before moving to Minneapolis. To her own surprise, she put down strong roots there. Now she lives in Minneapolis and wrangles her children, pets, and the mad scientist she keeps in the attic. When not writing or wrangling, she collects folk tales and photographs whatever stands still long enough to allow it. Discover more of her fiction at her website, **http://www.aswiebe.com**.

CPSIA information can be obtained
at www.ICGtesting.com
Printed in the USA
FFHW02n1909070818
47667114-51283FF